LADY COP

LADY COP

J.T. PRITCHARD

CUTTING EDGE

ISBN-13: 978-1-957868-45-5

Published by
Cutting Edge Books
PO Box 8212
Calabasas, CA 91372
www.cuttingedgebooks.com

To the
Gallant Police Women
on Duty
Throughout the World

CHAPTER ONE
THE MASHER

" A SINGLE?"

The usher was young and too thin for the wrinkled uniform. He blinked his flashlight toward the balcony stairs, and in its quick glow Peggy caught a glimpse of the young-old face, eyes beetle-like and knowing, lips pinched in a tight, secretive quirk. *I know you,* the face said. *I know what you are and what you're here for.*

She said, "Not too far front."

As he turned to lead the way down the cigarette-pocked carpeting, his glance met hers for an instant, full of challenge and watchfulness.

Often enough she had seen that same alerted look on the faces of the flashily dressed young punks in her own neighborhood, the ones her brother Duke hung out with, the ones who knew about her father and how she made her living now. In it was generally something of contempt, as well as amusement barely concealed:

I know you, copper. I know you and it stinks.

You'll slip, her own anger answered back. *Not yet, but some day, some day …*

Peggy picked her spot and moved into a seat separated by two empties from the man she had been watching for some time from the upper left corner of the balcony. In a few moments she heard a light cough and knew that Ada had taken a place two rows behind her.

She scarcely looked at the screen. The picture was an old print of something violently dull and typical of the cheap grind houses in those tawdry glittering blocks of mid-city, and she had already sat through it three times in the past week. In the glow of the projection beam flaring overhead, she watched the sparse afternoon audience.

There were the usual job-hunter types, come to seek forgetfulness after the morning's disappointments and still carrying their newspapers folded to the thumbed classified section. There were the poorly dressed young couples driven to those corners of dimness because there was no other place to take their need for affection's warmth in the chill unfriendliness of the city. There was an occasional lush, two steps removed from the wino gangs of Skid Row, sleeping off an early bout with the bottle. There were the prostitutes of both sexes, the prowlers out for whatever came along; the time-killers, and those who fell into no easy classification …

There also was the man two seats removed.

He was watching her now and sensing it from the corner of her eye, Peggy tried to appear interested in the picture. He cleared his throat, laughed heartily at a pratfall, trying to get her attention and possibly evoke some show of encouragement. He moved restlessly in his seat for a few minutes, while Peggy stared steadfastly ahead.

Her heart added an extra few beats to its rhythm. She knew it was silly to feel that stir of excitement. It was all routine. Everything ahead was charted, and she knew exactly what was going to happen. She wasn't going to feel very good about it, not while it was happening nor when it was all over, but it had to be that way. This work had been her choice, and this was a part of what she had become.

It's just a job, she kept telling herself. Every time she found herself in the midst of part of the world's nastiness, she tried to make herself believe that. While she played her part in these dirty little interludes, she sometimes whispered it under her breath. *Just a job!*

But it was more! You couldn't build a shell around yourself and live apart from what you did. You couldn't know filth and evil with part of yourself only.

No, it wasn't just a job at all. It was a way of life! But she went on doing it. And she knew that she would go on doing it tomorrow and the next day, just as she knew that she would go through with what she now had to do.

The man near her got up from his seat, scraping his feet, and moved over to the one next to her.

"Couldn't see over that fellow's head," he said in a half whisper of explanation.

Peggy ignored him. As he sat down, a corner of his trench coat fell partly across her lap. With a quiet brush of her hand she moved it aside, but as the man crossed his legs it again dropped over her side of the seat.

"Not much of a picture, is it?"

She gave no sign of having heard him. He was a younger man than she had thought him to be—in his mid-twenties, she guessed, and not too much older than she.

"Oh, the quiet type, eh?" He sighed deeply. "All right, be unfriendly, then."

For the next few minutes, nothing happened. Then, so slightly that she at first thought that she was imagining it, she began to feel the pressure of a knee against hers. She changed her position, but soon it was there again. This time she drew as far over from the man as was possible, glancing sharply at him as she did so. Undiscouraged, he sprawled lankily.

It was not long, now, until she felt the first creeping touch along her thigh. She glanced down. The trench coat was spilled over the armrest, partly on each seat; it moved slightly as his fingers, beneath its concealment, ran snakily over her skirt, gathering the material in tiny folds and drawing them upward.

Peggy turned squarely toward the man.

"You're too free with your hands, mister," she said.

He had leaned far to her side, and he had begun to whisper in a voice so low that only she could hear. Her mind tried to block out the stark obscenities as she looked around and caught Ada's eye. Ada nodded.

"... love it," he was saying. "You know you would. I'll bet you could show me ..."

"Mister," she said, "there's just one thing I can show you."

She opened her purse and flipped out a leather wallet. Even in that dim light she could see the deep flush of crimson that came over the man's face as he realized what he was looking at. He opened his mouth to speak, but Peggy shook her head.

"This isn't the place to talk about it," she said. "Let's go."

The man glanced nervously over his shoulder. A few people nearby had begun to get interested and were curiously watching. He shrugged and stood up. Peggy took his arm firmly and they went up the aisle, at the head of which Ada was now waiting. Ada fell in step on the man's other side, a pace behind.

"Listen," he said. "What is this, anyway? I didn't do anything ..."

"Just keep walking," Ada said. "You can do your explaining downtown."

"Some sort of a shake-down racket? Look, if you girls need money, I can understand that. I been hard up myself. Maybe I could even give you a little loan to help out, but ..."

He searched their faces, then addressed himself to Peggy.

"You just don't understand. I guess it was a mistake, trying to get acquainted with a girl in a movie, but you gotta understand! I just got in town about two months ago to get a job I heard about, and I don't know anybody. The job don't pay much, and Mom is sick, so I send most of my money home to her and Sis. That hardly leaves anything over after I pay my room rent and laundry and like that."

"Just walk," Ada ordered.

"Cripes, I even have to eat cold beans in my room sometimes, so I'll have carfare to get to work. I don't want you to think I feel sorry for myself, because Mom needs the money for medicine and all, but where does that leave me? I can't afford to go out to these gin mills, and I don't drink anyway, so where am I going to go to meet people? I don't mean just girls. I mean *anybody.*

"Maybe I get a little off the beam, sitting there in that room reading the paper, because you gotta talk to *somebody.* Hell, I can't even afford a radio. All I want is somebody to be friendly with, don't you understand?"

There were tears in his eyes by now. Peggy began to feel ill as she marched silently by his side.

"This will kill Mom," he said chokingly. "Just kill her. I've never been in trouble before—"

In mid-sentence he suddenly dropped to a crouch, breaking Peggy's grasp on his arm. He flailed his trench coat wildly in Ada's face, then raced for the stairs.

"Stop that man!" Peggy shouted at a uniformed figure just bending over the water fountain. As he turned, she saw that it was the usher she had previously encountered. From genuine surprise, his expression changed to one of slyness, followed by a false show of startled bewilderment.

"Say, what's the trouble here?" he demanded stupidly. "Whatcha trying to pull, you people?"

Without wasting further time, Peggy took off in pursuit of Ada and the sprinting man. Seemingly by accident, the usher now blundered into her path, blocking her way. She stiff-armed him aside just as Ada managed a runner's trip at the head of the stairs. The man tried to roll to the steps, but both women were on him before he could make it.

He winced as Ada's come-along bit metallically into his wrist.

"You!" Peggy snapped at the usher. "Get over here!"

The usher decided to be innocently puzzled this time.

"Manager's office," she said. "Walk behind this man. If he tries a break, you're expected to help stop him. This is an arrest."

"You're cops?" the usher asked. "Lady cops? Jeeze!"

"As if you didn't know," Peggy muttered under her breath.

"Gosh, if I'd known you was police ladies—"

"Can it," Ada said.

The manager was small and bald and excitable. He plucked nervously at a worn toothbrush moustache and did a little half-jig back and forth as Ada made the call to headquarters from his office.

"This is most regrettable," he said, anxiously. "Most regrettable, ladi—officers. You're quite certain, I suppose? I mean, there's no possibility that there was some sort of, ah, misunderstanding? I don't mean to imply that—well, it's very difficult to believe that anything like this could happen at the *Tivoli*."

"Is it?" Ada asked, arching one of her dark, rather heavy brows as she cradled the phone.

"There is no misunderstanding," Peggy said.

"Terrible," the manager said, shaking his head. "Simply terrible. It's a black eye all round, you know. Not just for me. For the entire staff. The owners—oh, the owners won't like this at all!"

"I shouldn't think they would," Ada remarked dryly. "A few more marks on the record, and the *Tivoli's* license stands a good chance of being pulled. Why don't you clean this joint up while you've still got a chance?"

The little manager glanced distastefully at the prisoner, who sat crying in one of the office chairs.

"You don't suppose we *want* to attract this sort of person, do you?" he said. "We police the place vigilantly, oh most vigilantly, I tell you! But an occasional bad egg will slip in and escape unnoticed. That could happen anywhere, in the best house in the city."

"Then how do you explain that constant parade of rouged boys along the cross-aisle of the balcony?" Peggy asked. "What do you think that's all about? What about those women standing in the back when there are plenty of empty seats? What are they waiting for?"

"Can't you just give me one break?" the man in the chair begged. "I never got into anything like this before. Look, I'll even get right out of town if you'll give me a break. I'll go back home where I know people, and get a job there—I'll see a doctor, if you think I ought to ..." He sobbed, face in hands. "But can't you see what you're doing if you put me in jail? Mom and Sis don't have a nickel ..."

"Oh, stop whining!" Ada snapped, impatiently. She looked at the usher, who was watching the prisoner as though fascinated. "We won't need you any more," she said.

"You can go back to your station, Willie," the manager added, authoritatively. "And—ah, don't mention any of this to the others just yet."

Willie grinned and slipped out.

The manager hesitated, then went to his desk and opened a drawer. He did something with a tin box, then fumbled with two envelopes. Finally he licked the envelopes closed and laid them on the scratched desk top.

"I just want to say, ladies, that the *Tivoli* appreciates what you are doing to keep the theatres of this city exactly what they ought to be—centers of clean and relaxing entertainment. Even though today's incident appears to reflect discredit on the *Tivoli* itself, I realize that your efforts are intended for the betterment of the entire industry. So—" He pushed the envelopes toward Ada. "—a small material token of that appreciation. It isn't much, but, frankly, the last few months ..."

The envelopes remained where they were.

"This wouldn't be a bribe, would it?" Ada asked quietly.

The manager gasped, then chuckled.

"You're joking, of course. It's merely that—well, sometimes one tends to forget just what police protection really means. Every day I read in the paper about some officer being injured or killed in the line of duty. I know you have some sort of benefit organization to help out in cases like that, but I rarely seem to read anything about private citizens or businessmen doing anything to help out."

"That's true enough," Ada said, guardedly.

"Well, I'd like to help out. That is, the *Tivoli* would like to help out. I don't know just how to make a contribution, but I'm sure you know how to get it into the proper hands. As for its being offered in any other spirit—absurd." His moustache survived another vigorous attack. "Of course, nothing would please me better than to hear that this unfortunate young man was simply the victim of some mistake, for neither he nor the *Tivoli* can well afford—"

"Mister," Ada said, "were you ever a member of the bar?"

"Why, no." The manager giggled, not quite sure whether he should be pleased.

"Well, you missed your calling. You ought to be running—vigilantly— with those ambulance chasers down around City Hall. You can take your envelopes, and whatever is in them, back. I'll give you the address of the Fund, and you can mail them in whenever you get around to it—if you don't forget."

The door to the office opened suddenly, and Ed Morretti from the prowl squad walked in with a foot patrolman.

"You got a package for downtown?" Morretti asked casually.

"Just a creep," Ada said, nodding.

"Frisked?"

"Clean, but you'd better make sure."

The prisoner was searched again, and Moretti started to lead him out.

"We'll follow you down," Ada called after him. He nodded without turning. The patrolman paused for a moment and studied Peggy.

"You must be new on the force, aren't you? I don't remember running into you."

Peggy nodded.

"First pinch?" he asked sympathetically.

"No, but it might just as well be."

"You look kind of rocky," he admitted.

"It's that man," she said. "The story he told. Every time I have to do something like this I feel rotten."

"Do something like what? He's a menace."

"Oh, it's his parents, his sister. And then you wonder whether you're not doing wrong, throwing a first offender in with a bunch of real case-hardened criminals."

The patrolman tipped his hat to scratch his head. "Well, I wouldn't know about that last," he said. "But I know something about this particular fella, because I helped bring him in twice before on this same beat. He's got a record of small stuff as long as your arm. By the way, what's your name, miss?"

"Malone. Peggy Malone." She was coloring with embarrassment at having been so naïve about the prisoner she had helped arrest.

"Malone. So, now, I used to know a cop by that name. You wouldn't be related, by any chance?"

"Big Mike Malone was my father."

The patrolman coughed and fiddled with the strap on his daystick.

"Well, I must be getting on, now. Good luck to you."

He left, and Peggy and Ada walked out into the lobby of the theatre, leaving the manager sitting tiredly at his desk.

"I'm a fool, Ada," Peggy said suddenly. "I'll never make out on the force. I just don't have what it takes."

"I guess we've all felt that way at first—and not just the women, either. After all, you've only been on six weeks. Give yourself a chance, kid."

Peggy shook her head.

"I can't make myself believe that people are really bad, that's the trouble. I'm a sucker for a sob story. Like the line this fellow was handing out."

"We're all suckers, Peggy," Ada told her, "until we realize that we're police, not judges or sociologists. Ever tell you what happened to me when I tried to make my first pinch on an 887? I ended up giving her five dollars that I really needed, and let her go. By the time I checked in, she'd been picked up again. She didn't have the five dollars—her pimp had it by that time, I guess."

"Check the john before we go?"

"Might as well."

They entered the door marked "Powder Room," and Peggy caught her breath against the sharp stench with its overlay of harsh antiseptic. She shuddered at the puddled litter, the crumbling plaster, and watched a huge, crippled cockroach scuttle under a broken tile. The place was empty.

"How do these theatres get away with it?" Peggy exclaimed.

Ada was touching up her lips before a cracked mirror, beneath which was scrawled, in purple lipstick, a crude drawing and an obscene invitation.

"I wouldn't know, kid," she said. "It's not my department. You guess. And fix your hair, copper."

Peggy hung her purse over her shoulder and stood at the washbowl next to Ada. Staring into the glass at her own green-blue eyes, she suddenly thought of a nursery rhyme.

"*... Can this be really me?*"

"Ada," she said, "why did you join the force? Why does *any* woman want a job like this?"

Ada pursed her lips over a facial tissue, turned her face to examine a tiny blemish on her dark cheek before she answered.

"That's a funny question," she finally said. "I suppose most of us just drifted into it. I mean—well, a lot of the wrens come from a family of cops, like you. They had some relative on the force, and they needed a job. Period."

"Yes, but it seems almost like wanting to be a female wrestler, or a welder or something. Your father—was he a cop?"

Ada slowly twisted her lipstick back in its case and closed it.

"No," she said. "No, my father wasn't a cop." She snapped her purse, and shifted her shoulder under the weight of the .32 Smith & Wesson she was carrying in a shoulder rig under her suit jacket. Then she turned to Peggy.

"Let's put it on the road, kid."

As they passed the candy counter, Willie, the usher, was lolling in indolent conversation with the flashy blonde girl who ran it. Peggy hesitated, then walked over to him.

She said without preliminary, "That bit of business you pulled upstairs was interference with an officer. No, don't bother to look injured. You knew what was going on. I just want to warn you—an attitude like yours eventually pays off the hard way. Better straighten that out now, Willie, because sooner or later …"

She left the sentence dangling and went back to join her partner. It was a bit silly, she thought, and useless—even though she felt better for having got it off her chest; she still thought like a schoolteacher. She was still a long way from being a real cop, hard and competent, like Ada.

On the other hand, she was a long way from Paris, which was the way she wanted it. Not that Paris hadn't been fun …

CHAPTER TWO
FRENCH FORAY

THE SONGS all glorified Paris in springtime; even in late July, Peggy Malone—American high-school teacher of history and first-year French—found it exciting, delightful, fabulous. As she hurried up the two flights to her little apartment, she hummed a tune some children had been singing at the corner of the cobbled street.

It wasn't exactly a Hollywood musical director's conception of a Parisian street scene, but it was Peggy's Paris and she was in love with it. In those weeks she was a little bit in love with everybody and everything, including the landlady's cat that now accompanied her into the apartment and trotted to the bowl of milk which was waiting. And with one particular somebody she was more than a little in love. Or thought she was. It was hard to be certain, because she had never been in love before.

Jacques Dubois was her own age plus a few months, and one of the first people to whom she had been introduced after her arrival in France. He worked in his father's import-export office.

His English was perhaps somewhat better than her French. He had grown up in Paris, but had prowled it with the searching thoroughness of, for instance, a young mid-western poet just discovering New York. Their first afternoon's excursion had taken them from the Jardin des Plantes, where comfortable burghers properly shepherded their families on a grave Sunday stroll, to shadowed cave-like bistros where students and artists argued the finer points of existentialism and Swedish jazz in an atmosphere of candlelight, tobacco smoke, and vin ordinaire. Afterward Peggy and he had spent more and more time together.

They had strolled the Boul' Mich', window-shopped the Rue de la Paix, peered down the narrow alley which was the Street of the Fishing Cat. There had been the day on the Ile de la Cité, where Peggy had bought a caged finch only to release it, and whence they had returned with armfuls of flowers which had caused an amiable, bantering commotion on the Metro. There had been *aperitifs* at sidewalk cafés where pale-faced girls slowly sipped their pernods and waited for someone to offer to take care of the accumulated saucers. There had been the Folies Bergere and the Moulin Rouge and *escargots* at a three-tabled restaurant where the chef, between orders, sat tailor-legged in a corner and knitted squares of an afghan allegorizing Ahab's quest for Moby Dick.

And eventually there had been the day spent at the little country inn a few kilometers from the city, where the proprietor provided them with long cane poles to fish the river, and later cooked and served them their catch. It was on that day, as they rested under a tree in the apple orchard, that Jacques had first kissed her.

That had not surprised her. Most of the men she had known had tried to, sooner or later, and the ones she liked had succeeded. In fact, few of them had waited as long as Jacques, which seemed to give the lie to certain traditions concerning Gallic impetuosity. No, what truly surprised her was the intensity with which she had found herself returning his kiss. Within moments, lying in the sparkling kaleidoscopic pattern of sunlight as it filtered through the leaves, the sweet fruity smell of the orchard mingling with the hay-like odor of the high grasses which crushed beneath her restless thighs and twisting shoulders as Jacques' weight began to add itself to hers, she realized that she was on the brink of giving herself.

Trembling and troubled, she had slipped from his arms and darted away, as frantic as the startled hare which scurried from her path. Jacques had not pursued her, nor even called after her. When, out of breath and feeling rather foolish, she had rested at a rail fence, he simply walked to her side and quietly suggested that they go back to the inn.

Since then—well, since then there had been something more. There had been long evenings in her apartment when, after the meal she prepared had been eaten and the dishes put away, she and Jacques would sit and talk about themselves and each other and the bright limitless world that exists for the eyes of lovers to see. Eventually they would find themselves in each other's arms, on the couch with the loosened spring which twanged protestingly at exactly the wrong moments.

But always, just when it seemed that physical yearning could be put off no longer, when her own passion's hunger neared the point of no control, Peggy had hesitated—and drawn back.

"I've got to be *sure,* Jacques!" she had exclaimed the first time. "I've never ... Well, I'm sorry if I disappoint you, but I could never make love just ... just *pour le sport.* With me it's got to mean ... everything."

And Jacques, though his hands were nervous as he lighted cigarettes for both of them, had quietly replied, "We will wait until you are sure." And he had turned to tune the radio.

There had been no talk of marriage—and for that Peggy only respected Jacques the more. It would have been an easy bribe, a cheap bribe for one who was trifling. Jacques, she knew, would never put out the bait of promised respectability to further a casual affair. And neither would he suggest marriage to a woman who did not love him enough to come to him without it. Not that they had ever discussed these matters directly; she simply understood that this was a part of his personal code, as she understood so many things about him.

Sometimes she felt that she understood herself far less. She had never thought of herself as living by any formalized set of rules, and yet she realized that her present actions were guided by some sort of deeply ingrained ethical sense. If Jacques were the right man for her, then she would go to him completely, without reservation, in any circumstance. But if he were not—well, she did not want to carry the memory of past mistakes to the right man when she did find him, nor have less than all of herself to offer. What she felt could have been best summarized, perhaps, by a remark her father had made to her once.

She had been fifteen then, beginning to use a touch of lipstick, and old Mike, taking note of the frilly wisps of lace and silk which were making their first appearance on the clothesline, had shown a trace of worry natural to a man who had tried to be both mother and father to two children and was not quite sure that he had succeeded.

"I know you're a level-headed kid, Peg," he had told her. "You've had to be, to be left on your own as much as you have. And I hope you can stay level, because I want you to be a happy woman. I'm not going to preach or give you a long-winded speech. There's one rule of thumb, though, that's pretty practical, even if it does sound corny: *Never go to bed with anybody whose toothbrush you wouldn't be willing to share.*"

"I'll remember that, Mike," she had said. "But you don't have to worry. I'm not going to bed with anybody I wouldn't want to look at over the breakfast table for the rest of my life."

And she had rumpled his salt-and-pepper hair and tossed him the evening paper.

The question now was, why did she still hesitate? She knew very well that she would share a toothbrush with Jacques if that unlikely necessity were to arise. And she had never been sur-feited with his companionship, so the breakfast-table test could undoubtedly be passed. There was something deeper, something she didn't understand, something which would not allow her to relax as she should. She wished that she could talk to Mike about it. But then, if she had, he would simply have listened while she talked herself out and, refusing to interfere, leave her to make her own decision.

Standing at her window and looking out over the angled roofs and chimney pots, Peggy know that for her own peace of mind, as well as Jacques', she must come to a decision soon. They both deserved to know where they stood in this matter. If there were something constitutionally wrong in their relationship, if she were somehow psychically unable to accent physical love, it would be better to know it at once, so that friendship at least might be salvaged.

It would have to be tonight.

A glance at the mantle clock, and she hurried into the bath-room to light the heater for her bath. She would just have time for that and a few small household chores before Jacques arrived with groceries for the dinner they had planned—an errand which he insisted on performing, since he pretended to be sure that she would allow herself to be cheated at the markets, like all the rich Americans. As though, she thought wryly, a girl who had taken over many of the responsibilities of a woman when she was ten would not know the value of a fat hen anywhere, whether it cackled in French or English. She had told him all about herself and her circumstances, of course.

"My father is a cop—*un flic*," she had told him. She had paused, trying to equate Big Mike with the local *gendarmerie* who, in their flaring cloaks and flat box caps, always gave the impression of being rather undersized. And then she had added, "An honest cop."

Mike Malone was an honest cop, all right—in a city where a policeman's paycheck seemed always to lag behind in the race with spiraling living costs. That was why Peggy and her kid brother—christened Girard, but called "Duke" by everyone—had grown up in a railroad flat in the "Bloody Twelfth" on the South Side, had gone to P.S. 42—"The Rat Hole"—and had early learned the little niceties of saving a penny here and a penny there when it came to buying for the family larder. That was why, Peggy sometimes bitterly thought, the girl who had been Marie Castellani before she married the huge, raw-boned Irishman and bore his two children, died so early—and so old. If only there had been money for the operation when it was first needed, if the doctor's warning had not been kept a secret from Mike, put aside in favor of a hundred and one other pressing needs ...

Peggy marked the end of her childhood with that last Christmas of bittersweet memory, when she had been ten and Duke five. For only a few short weeks later she was trying to cope with many of the problems of running a real household.

And she remembered that there had been problems aplenty. At first sympathetic relatives came to help out occasionally, but they had their own lives to live, families of their own. Once, for a few days, there had been a vague cousin from another city, a reddish-faced, plump woman in her late thirties. On the day she had arrived, a bottle of cooking sherry had appeared on the kitchen shelf; and everyday thereafter the bottle had to be replaced—something Mike never knew. Nor did he know of the afternoon when the woman had taken Peggy on her soft lap, opened her own sweat-smelling blouse, and tried to persuade the girl to fondle her large, thick-nippled breasts. Peggy had simply told her father that she did not like her cousin, and the woman had left after a scene of bitter spitefulness and a prediction that Peggy would come to a bad end.

With the aid of an occasional housekeeper, things had been managed, somehow. As time passed, the circumstances of the little family gradually became easier, more secure. Even college became first a possibility, then a reality. And now as though by a miracle, she was in France, with the noble city of Paris proving itself all that she had promised herself it would be. And that was a great deal, because it had to live up to five years of promises.

It had been that long ago, while she was still in college, that she had begun making plans and setting aside small sums toward the trip. And, of course, discussing it with Mike.

She always discussed things with him, as she had when the two of them were battling to keep their little household together. Plans, hopes, problems—the two of them would sit down together and take them apart, then rearrange the pieces. And somehow, when they got through, the practical mechanisms of things always seemed to work better.

But Mike was almost four thousand miles away, aside from the fact that she knew that her present problem was one she must solve by herself. More than that—she wondered if her emotional difficulty might not be really tied up with Mike, stem from the abnormal situation which had made their relationship something more than the usual one between father and daughter. They had been close, not only in those areas of domestic life which ordinarily concern husband and wife—questions of the budget, the bank balance, and whether the living-room furniture should be reupholstered or replaced—but also in matters which are generally the subject of private discussion between mother and daughter. All of which made for a possibility which had to be considered and, if existent, rectified. She wasn't alarmed by the thought—merely troubled, and curious. After all, she had taken a few psychology courses in college, and she knew that things like that happened and could be adjusted. Certainly something had so far prevented her from consummating her affair with Jacques. And she loved Jacques at least as much as most women love the men to whom they give themselves.

Well, tonight she would try, really try to break past that wall of restraint. Even if it meant a sort of white lie to Jacques, even if she had to *force* herself to go through with it. For that way she could at least learn if she were, essentially, only half a woman. It didn't sound very romantic, and she was sorry about that. She would have to keep Jacques from suspecting that she was not coming to him quite artlessly, out of simple response to his love. Whatever else, he must believe in her passion. Although a virgin, she was not an ignorant girl, nor wholly unsophisticated, and even a woman who is frigid can simulate.

As, a few minutes later, she stretched one slim, naked leg over the edge of the tub to toe the water, she began to count the ways.

CHAPTER THREE
LOVE POSTPONED

THE LANDLADY'S CAT mewed at the door, and Jacques, who had been listening to the American baseball scores on the radio, went to let it out.

"Dem bums!" he said, as the latest Dodgers' catastrophe was announced. He pronounced it "bombs."

"But wait until *next* year," Peggy promised.

Crossing the room, he paused behind the chair on which she was sitting, legs curled beneath her, and touched her dark hair. Her hand was quick to find his, and with a nuzzling, affectionate stroke of her cheek she turned to kiss his fingers.

"Always next year," he said. "Always I lose money."

"Brooklyn is a fine team to root for, but not to bet on," she told him.

"I have been learning this. The Paris correspondents for the New York papers have been educating me at odd evens."

"Even odds."

"However you say it. It means that they always win."

"Only a sucker bets on the other guy's game. You ought to know that."

"Yes," he sighed, "but I just do not convince myself that baseball is not my game. Do you know, when I was fifteen I could tell you the batting averages of all the principal players for three years back?"

"What makes you think I would have been interested?"

"But all Americans like baseball! It said so in a book I read once, one that the government put out when the American Army was in Paris. Hot dogs, it said. Apple pie and ice cream. Peanuts and Coca Cola. Nash Kelvinator and kill the umpire. Mom's turkey hash and Pop's six shares of American Telephone and Telegraph. I know all about it. The book said—"

"You are just a little bit crazy. You know that, don't you?"

"Just enough to get by."

"But nice. Very nice."

He buried his face in her hair, breathing its fragrance.

"Such softness ..." he murmured. "I never knew hair could be so delightful ... soft as the morning sun ..."

His moods were volatile; he might be banteringly gay one moment, intense and serious an instant later. The pulse of emotion was, in Peggy, more steady, slower to alter.

"Aw, shucks," she said. "Tell me about my purty eyes, mister."

"I don't know about your eyes. Sometimes they are blue. As blue, almost, as the wing of ... of ... *les papillons*—flutterby? And again—green, like the eyes of the cat."

He moved around her chair and sat on its arm. Lightly he touched her chin, turning her face to his kiss. She could feel his thigh, tense and hard, tremble slightly against her forearm; her fingers clutched his knee as his lips sought hers more and more intimately, as their mouths became more nearly one. A sudden start jerked through her shoulders, convulsive and involuntary. Her cheek twitched nervously as her lips first resisted, then accepted his probing tongue.

Even then her mind was busy, questioning. In the very instant that passion was quickening, as her body began its subtle response, she wondered at herself. No man had even stirred her as Jacques did; never had her own need for fulfillment echoed so strongly to that urging plea of male love. And yet something within her was hesitant, protesting with a small voice which, she already knew, would grow more insistent as her pent-up emotions demanded their natural outlet. Through her loins she could feel a suffusing warmth, spreading outward from a burning core, so nearly tangible that she could almost measure its inching progress. And yet ... and yet ...

Jacques' fingers, which had lain against his cheek, moved down along the throbbing contour of her throat, caressing the swelling-muscled outline with a gentle kneading, almost as a sculptor might tenderly work the clay of a figure he loved.

"Amante ... précieux ..."

His hand touched flutteringly across the swell of her breast, found the V of her dress and slipped inward. Her nipples tightened, pressed to his warm palm, as she again sought his kiss. His fingers curled, cradled the soft weight which trembled slightly with each pounding heartbeat.

"A dove," he said softly. "I hold a frightened white dove ..."

He drew back then, and their eyes met, locked. Moments dripped away into a tiny eternity as he silently questioned, while she tried to look deeper into him, to find, perhaps, some answer of her own. Then she took his hand, kissed the rather slender wrist with its curling sprinkle of hair, and stood up.

He watched her cross the room and snap out a light, leaving the room illuminated only by a single, rose-shaded table lamp in one corner. She went to the door and threw its latch, then returned to a spot almost exactly in the center of the room, where that afternoon she had placed a small scatter rug she had purchased. There was an air of formality, ritual, nearly, in her actions, as though she had already rehearsed, at least mentally, what she now did.

Without looking at Jacques, and without a word, she unfastened the snaps along the side of her dress, pulled the bow of its belt, and slipped it over her head. The dress fell, a crumpled pile, at her feet, while she ran her fingers through her hair to settle its disarray. In the breathless hush of the room, the ubiquitous horn of a taxi intruded blatantly.

Her fingers fumbled the hooks of her brassiere—a film of lace obviously incapable of any support, the lack of which was of no concern to Peggy's youthful firm-toned figure. It slid from her arms and dropped atop the dress. The quick intake of breath as Jacques half stood, then sat back again, was like a stabbing shout in the silence.

Peggy's glance flickered toward him from half-lowered lids. She hooked a thumb under the band of the canary yellow panties which clung so closely to her full hips, beginning to push the garment down along her lithe flank.

And then she stopped dead, standing still as a statue for a dozen ticks of the mantle clock.

All her senses seemed hyperactive. She was aware of the whispered creakings of the old house; she could hear the beat of her own heart, and its heavy pressure throbbed in her ears.

She had to force her hand to obey her, now. Her sheer undergarment moved downward another revealing inch ... another ...

He'll think I'm teasing, her mind said in a sort of panic. *He mustn't think I'm pretending coyness, doing a fancy strip-act ...*

She bit her lip to the point of sharp pain, trying to gather strength with which to fight herself. She needed—she needed ... Would a drink help?

Abruptly she turned and walked to the kitchen, heels loudly tapping on the bare floor, stooping in a half-kneeling position to clatter amongst the contents of an under-shelf cabinet.

It isn't shame, she was thinking. *I'm not ashamed of my body or its demands. And if Jacques wanted to paint me, instead of those still-lifes he does as a hobby—if he wanted to have me as a model,*

I wouldn't feel this way about being naked in front of him. And it can't be conscience, because I know that Jacques is good, that my feeling for him is clean ... Then what is it?

Her hand was shaking so that she spilled some of the liquor over the sides of the two pony glasses on the black lacquered tray. She wiped the brandy up carefully, taking longer than the job required, then returned to the room where Jacques waited.

"Armagnac, monsieur?" She tried to be flippant; somehow she saw that beneath Jacques' answering smile he was troubled for her. Her conduct was out of character; he knew that she was a virgin, for she had told him so, and he knew that only some tremendous emotional strain could have driven her into a state of mind where she was making a kind of burlesque of an experience which, to a girl of her sensitivity, should have been a moment of deep, almost religious meaning.

It is not thus that lovers should come to each other, and into the situation there had entered such a strong factor of the unnatural that it bordered on perversion. He was thinking that little games and amusements may have their place in a relationship of long standing, may add piquancy and an intriguing novelty to marital familiarity. But there is something seriously out of place in the picture of a girl who, offering herself for the first time, approaches that moment as though it were but a matter of light diversion. The tableau they made—Jacques reaching for a cigarette which a few minutes before he had dropped, forgotten, into the ashtray, his London-cut business suit neat and almost formal; Peggy naked from the waist up, wearing open-toed pumps, fine-gauge hose held by rosetted garters which accentuated the bareness of her thighs and ran upward to her hips, where the narrow, cut-away belt was plainly visible under the nearly transparent panties—was a travesty which might well have been an illustration torn from the pages of a salacious magazine. And of this they were both aware, which made the situation even more difficult. And they both knew that it was wrong.

Jacques took the glass of brandy. He did not want it—there was only one thing he wanted at that moment—but he had intuitively guessed that Peggy really needed, or thought she needed, a drink, and he made a show of being pleased. Still she stood there, holding the tray at the height of her bare waist, smiling falsely in imitation of the cigarette girl in a cabaret.

"Something else, monsieur?"

He looked at her standing so before him, hair somewhat tousled, undergarment still askew at her hip, and his face colored.

"No. No, nothing else."

She put down the tray and took her own pony glass, using both hands. Even then she spilled a few drops as she tossed it down. Jacques touched his glass to his lips, then put it aside.

I'm spoiling it all, her mind told her. *I wanted simply to undress for him, naturally, go to him with my love ... But this ...*

"Come here," he said suddenly.

She took the two steps to his side, not knowing what he wanted or what he was going to do, but knowing that whatever it was, she must now accede. He took both her hands in his, kissed them. Then, as he let them drop, his arms encircled her waist, fingers fondling while they moved slowly over the curve of her spine, over the swell of her hips. At his touch, prickles ran along the length of her thighs, stirring the tiny, almost invisible dusting of fine hair into brief, restless life.

"No!" she exclaimed in a throaty whisper. "No, I—"

He looked steadily at her, and she quieted.

"I'm sorry," she said. "I really want you to. I *need* you to."

She waited for what was going to happen next. Nothing happened. Jacques simply continued to look at her, coveting her with his eyes, his face a mixture of love and strain.

"Please," she finally said. "Please."

And now he apparently decided that he too needed a drink, for he paused long enough to take it in one quick swallow. Then he rose and picked her up. Cradling her in his arms, nuzzling her throat and lips with his lips, he carried her to the couch.

But just as he was about to take his pleasure of her warm, sweet flesh, there came a gentle knock at the door.

They both tried to ignore it.

Then the light tapping at the door became more imperative, and Peggy turned restlessly in Jacques' arms. The Fates themselves seemed to be in conspiracy against the consummation of their love.

"I'll have to answer," she whispered. "The landlady knows we're in."

He nodded and released her, sitting up and mopping his brow with a quick, backhand swipe of his hand. His necktie had been loosened and was somewhat twisted; aside from that, after a few swift adjustments he was still dressed as though for a business conference. Peggy slipped from the couch like a prisoner reprieved from the gallows at the last instant.

"Yes," she called, as the knock came again. "What is it?"

"A telephone call, miss. Very important."

"It can't be that important. Ask for the name and I'll call back."

"It is the foreign operator to whom I spoke. There is a call from America. The party will speak only to you."

"America! I—I'll be right down."

As she stepped to a closet for her dressing robe, she turned to Jacques with a frown.

"A transatlantic call. I can't imagine …"

She hurriedly tied the belt of the quilted robe, stepped into slippers.

"Shall I come with you?"

She shook her head, laughed without conviction. "It's probably just a surprise. There's a party or something, and they've decided to phone me. You know how people are at parties."

But, like a leaden weight in her chest was a premonition of disaster. It was no one calling from a party in America. In America the hour was—she couldn't remember, exactly, but it was still early evening.

She hurried down the stairs to the hall phone. The landlady, impressed by the importance of such an occasion, hovered at the doorway of the parlor, became embarrassed by her own curiosity and withdrew, leaving the door slightly ajar.

The short time that it took to make the connection was interminable. There were odd cracklings, voices that spoke in several languages, in codes of numbers; briefly she was in contact with a man from Berlin who was trying to raise someone in Dijon. The French telephone system, she thought, certainly deserved its reputation as being the worst in Europe.

New York responded; she heard a relay to a small town in Vermont by way of Albany, and then Chicago was on the wire for a few seconds. Suddenly she was aware of an entire world of communication struggling and working across the seas, tying the earth together in a network of wires and cable, busily probing through the intricacies of the spider-web system man had spun.

And then, thin and wavering at first, but eventually full and clear as though the call had come from around the corner, from the shop of the *boucher* where skinned rabbits hung with their forepaws still furred as proof that they were not cats, she heard a familiar voice, heard a name she knew.

It was an accident, but not an accident. It was an illness, but not an illness. It was many ambiguous things which it was not.

The voice was that of Tom Flanagan, a long-time friend of her father, an important figure in the political machinations which centered about City Hall.

The message was Death.

Afterward, when she had automatically, dully, agreed to the things which the voice suggested, after she had spoken of plane schedules and arrangements for the funeral, she went back up the stairs. She had never been aware of the banister before; now she clung to its smooth, hand-worn unevenness through both flights. The steps creaked beneath her weight. She had never noticed that before either.

Jacques was standing at a window. He turned eagerly, then saw her expression.

"My father is dead," she said. "My father is dead and I must go back to America to bury him."

The words sounded artificial. The situation was unreal, with the unreality of nightmare. She could not yet believe that what she had just heard was true.

"Mike is dead," she said. "Dead. Mike. My father."

She took off her robe and dropped it on a chair. Her nakedness was now of no importance. Hardly aware of what she did, she began to pick up her scattered clothing.

"Your father ... dead?" Jacques said. "I ... I don't know what to say."

"There isn't anything to say. He's dead. That's all of it."

"But ..."

"They called me from America. He was a strong man, a healthy man. I don't understand."

Jacques studied her, his face concerned and anxious.

"How can I help?" he asked.

"No one can help. I must go back. The flight reservation has been taken care of. I leave in the morning. What time is it?"

He glanced at his watch and told her the hour.

"Good. That will leave me time to—to do the things I must do. I must pack, I must—will you speak to the landlady for me?"

"Of course. But Peggy—"

"Yes?"

"Shouldn't I ... I mean, I could take leave and come with you. Shouldn't I do that?"

"No. There is no reason."

"There is reason. I love you, and you have grief."

"It wouldn't be right. Not for us. When we spoke of you taking a trip to America some day, we were talking of something that would be gay, something that would be fun. I wanted to show you—oh, so many, many things! And I wanted you to meet Mike, and my kid brother. If you came now, I would have no heart for anything. The very fact of your presence would be a constant reminder of—of my father's absence. You do understand, don't you?"

"Not wholly. But I am sure you know what is right for you and what you must do. That is enough."

She hung up the dress in a closet, took out one which was simple and black. The open-toed shoes were put away and a sober, sensible pair she used for walking were found. The transparent panties and the filmy hose she took into the bathroom. There would be time for them to dry if they were washed immediately. She could not have worn them now; they were wholly inappropriate, in themselves and also by association.

She was at the chest of drawers, selecting substitutes, when the landlady again came to the door. Peggy had not closed it completely, it was off balance on its worn hinges, and it swung open at the touch of the woman's knock.

"Your pardon, child ..."

The landlady was a practical person who had learned many things in her lifetime. She nodded gravely at Jacques, giving no hint of surprise at the scene she had come upon.

"I could not help but hear, downstairs, the telephone call. If there is something I can do ..."

"You are very kind." Peggy was still dry-eyed; her grief had not yet broken, for she was even yet in that initial state of numbing shock. "There is nothing. I need only pack and be ready for the plane in the morning. I am sorry that I must leave without notice, but perhaps you can rent the apartment again, before my month's rent is up."

"I am not concerned with such as that." The landlady waved a hand in impatient gesture. "Nor, under the circumstances, can I accept the full rental. Tonight I will see how much should be paid for the time you have been here, and before you leave I will have ready the balance which is due you."

"I cannot take it. It is good of you to offer, but our agreement was—"

"This is not a time to speak of agreements and make arguments. One does not try to turn a profit from another's distress. The money will be waiting. But is there no way in which I can be of assistance? The packing, perhaps?"

"Thank you. I want to do that myself. I want to keep busy."

"I am sorry, very sorry, for your loss. And in any case, I would regret having you leave. When you are in Paris again, I hope that you can be my tenant."

After a few more words she nodded once more to Jacques and left. It was only then that Peggy realized that all the time they had been talking she had been standing there stark naked, a pair of stockings dangling from her hand. It seemed impossible that she could have been unaware of that, and yet it had happened. And, somehow, it was of no importance whatsoever. If anything, it was amusing, and she began to giggle.

"Stop that," Jacques said quietly.

She caught herself, forced herself to calmness. From a drawer she took a plain white garter belt, fastened it about her waist, and sat down on a cane chair to put on her stockings. Watching her as she stretched out one slender leg to straighten the seam, Jacques echoed the landlady, seeming to muse over the words:

"When you are in Paris again ..."

Peggy stepped into a pair of cotton panties, smoothed them snugly about her hips. She reached for a brassiere, but he interrupted her before she slipped it on.

"Only a moment," he said. "I want to look at you. I want to remember you."

She felt a touch of impatience. Sex was now the least of matters in her mind, and she wondered that he should have the bad taste to be concerned with it at such a time.

"There will be another night, other rooms."

He shook his head, and the corners of his mouth were quirked with his own sadness.

"There will not be another night, nor another room. Not for us."

"I will be back. I am coming back."

"Not to me."

"To you."

"No. I would like to believe that, but I know it is not so. If we had been to bed together a week ago—if the phone message had been delayed, perhaps ..." He rose and went to her, took her face in his hands and tenderly, chastely almost, kissed her forehead. "I have loved you very much," he said. "And because I love you, I sense this fact. You may return to France. We may see each other and even be friends again. But we cannot meet as lovers. It is better for us both to accept this, rather than pretend that it can be otherwise. Tonight will have left us too conscious of its interruption. We could not ever again make love without remembering, without you reliving its sorrow. Had our love been complete, you would want me to be with you now, you would need me. But now your thought is not of us, of any future we might have. You think of your brother, and home to you is still a place in the States, not simply whatever place in which we two find ourselves together. I am sorry that it should be this way—that I cannot make myself believe that this is an interruption and not an ending. For I have loved you very, very much, my darling."

"And I—I—" She had to pause, to draw a deep, sobbing breath. "I have loved you too, Jacques."

Then, at last, she was crying.

CHAPTER FOUR
PISTOL GRIP

" I CAN'T BELIEVE IT," Peggy said. "I try to make myself understand that he's gone, now, but I keep expecting him to open the door and … and …"

She looked distractedly about the living room of the second-floor flat, at the wheat-patterned wallpaper of which Mike had been so dubious when she had selected it, at the scarred window-sill where Duke had tried to cut his initials with his first pen-knife; she remembered as though it had happened yesterday the accident with an ink bottle which had permanently marked the table where she and her brother had studied. A hundred memories whispered back at her, and she turned to Duke, who was sitting on the sofa with his hands clasped between his knees, wondering if he, too, felt the presence of that place, the wash of memory. He was staring into space, his expression adolescently unreadable, and he did not look up.

Tom Flanagan, his ruggedly handsome face grave, nodded understandingly.

"I know. It doesn't seem possible. We were friends all our lives. His parents and mine came to this country on the same boat, moved to this city together. We grew up next door to each other. I guess you two know that story by heart."

He shook his massive head. His hair, thick as that of a man in early youth, was snow-white, combed straight back in deep waves. When he was in his teens a single, inch-wide streak of gray had appeared in hair that was coal black; within two years it had spread until the last vestige of its original color was gone. And then, as though Nature, grown capricious, had also become bored and had forgotten him, the passage af years had scarcely touched him. Muscles had thickened, the line of jowl had grown more distinct, but the tone of skin remained fresh and pinkish and firm; his motions were decisive and sure, bespeaking the unslowed reactions which directed them; the shrewd eyes were crystal clear, and sharp as the mind behind them.

"I was with him the night you were born, Peggy. I'll never forget that night. He kept pacing the floor of the hospital waiting room, vowing that when he was sure everything was all right he was going to look for a speakeasy, forget he was a cop, and get roaring drunk. But that wasn't the way it turned out. When you finally arrived, and he'd seen your mother and blarneyed a nurse into giving him a non-regulation peek at you, I took him off to a place I know. I guess that must have been the only time in his life that Mike was in a blind pig, except on a raid. Anyway, he sat there and grinned at himself in the bar mirror and *I* got drunk. The way it ended up, I finally drank the one whiskey he'd had in front of him for an hour, and he took me home and poured me into bed. And damned if he didn't make a report on the place next day. That was Mike."

"The room is strange," Peggy said. "Mike's chair is gone. And there's a different rug."

The question in her voice was directed to her brother. He raised his veiled stare to her, then nodded shortly toward Tom.

"Ask him. He took care of that. I just sleep here."

The older man frowned slightly, then cleared his throat.

"Look, Duke … Take is easy, will you? I know you're upset. We're all upset. Let's try not to make it any harder for each other."

"What is it?" Peggy asked. "I don't know what you two are talking about."

Tom threw an exasperated glance at the boy, drew a breath to fortify himself against an unpleasant task.

"The accident, Peg. It was ... You understand. It left—evidence. I had the chair destroyed, and I had this rug brought in from my home to replace the other. It would have been impossible to have—to get rid of—the stains."

She understood, then. A thirty-eight slug at short range was messy. What it could do to a man's head wasn't pleasant to think about. A spatter of blood and bone and tissue. The first gush of blood from the gaping hole, then the steady, slowing drip over clothing and self, soaking in a widening stain when it reached the rug.

"I'm sorry," Tom said. "I had hoped that you wouldn't notice immediately, but of course that was foolish."

She stared at the place where Mike's comfortable chair had stood, at that part of the rug which must cover a rust-colored mark, all of Mike that was left in that room.

"They've got to replaster the ceiling downstairs," Duke said abruptly. "The blood—"

"Shut up, Duke," Tom Flanagan snapped.

"But he was so *careful* with firearms," Peggy said. "When Duke and I were small he walloped both our bottoms for breaking into the gun cabinet one afternoon, even though all we were after was some oil for Duke's bike—"

"We weren't so young," Duke interjected. "I got that bike for my tenth birthday, so you were fifteen."

"—and the ammunition was locked up in a box in his bureau. Every night, when he came home in uniform, the first thing he did was break his revolver and unload it. When he took us down to the police range and taught us how to shoot—"

"He didn't even like me to point a pop-gun at anybody, not even at a stray dog that was dirtying the front steps," Duke remembered. " 'Never aim a gun at anyone or anything that you don't expect to kill', was the way he said it."

"So an accident like that—it's almost incredible," Peggy continued. "He'd handled guns for a long time, yes. But he never grew casual about them, or careless. He knew that it's always the unloaded gun that kills. And when he did clean a revolver—or his shotgun when he'd been out for ducks—it was always in the kitchen, where he could lay out the parts on the table. In here he'd have had to spread papers around, and that would have been a nuisance he wouldn't have put up with."

The man who had been for so many years her father's friend had put his hand to his forehead, so that she could not see his eyes, but he nodded in reluctant agreement, as though this were a conclusion to which he had known she would come, knew the inevitable question she must now ask.

"Tom. It wasn't an accident, was it? He wasn't cleaning that revolver. He deliberately shot himself. That's what you've been trying to keep from me, isn't it?"

His expression was now tired and drawn, as though the effort of maintaining a pretence had weighed heavily. He rubbed his fingers across his eyes, then down one close-shaven cheek.

"I can't answer that, Peggy. I honestly don't know. Nobody can know. He didn't leave any note, if that can help you answer the question. And there wasn't anything to indicate that it was wholly accidental, either. He wasn't cleaning the revolver; that much is clear. It was fully loaded, with the exception of the one bullet that—that was fired. It was still held in his right hand when he was found."

Peggy's whole self was a seething mass of protest against this new knowledge. Mike, a suicide? It wasn't possible; he had been too vital, too strongly aware of life's meaning for that. Unless ...

"Was he sick, Tom? Had he learned something about himself that meant it would be better for him to—to go quickly?"

"I thought of that. Doc Ferrier gave him a routine check-up less than a month ago. Sound as a dollar."

"But—"

"For Christ's sake!" Duke's voice was harsh and angry. "Why do you keep beating around the bush this way? Why don't you tell her the truth?" He jumped up and strode the length of the room, wheeled with a quick violence, his mouth twisted with bitterness. "You've been running this show, Mr. Flanagan. Are you going to finish it, or do you want me to explain it to her?"

Peggy looked from him to the older man, bewildered and, somehow, feeling fright.

"What is it?" she asked. "What is it that you two are trying to say—or trying not to say? I have a right to know! I've sensed something from the beginning, something that was being covered up, and I have a right to know what it is. I won't be treated this way! I'm not a child. Nothing that concerns Mike should be a secret from me!"

"They're working on him now at the funeral parlor, trying to get his face into shape so that we can look at it tomorrow, do you know that?" Duke spoke quietly, but his eyes were a sunken snarl. "They came around asking for a photograph. A photograph, so they'd know what to make it look like."

"Duke. Please." Tom Flanagan's voice was strong, with the soft determination of a man who is accustomed to being obeyed. "We are all under strain. You aren't helping."

"I'm sorry. I mean, I guess I'm sorry."

"I have to know ..."

"It was probably coincidence," Tom Flanagan said, with a kind of helplessness, as he faced Peggy's grief again.

Duke snorted.

"Tell her, then," he said. "You've been the big operator. You moved in on the act as soon as it happened. You phoned her, you fixed up the flight schedule for her, you tipped the taxi driver when we drove to the field, you bought the cup of coffee you thought I needed while we were waiting. Hell, you even made the funeral arrangements. Don't stop now."

Tom seemed to be studying the youth as he reached into his breast pocket and took out a silver cigar case. He showed no anger, or even annoyance, at that direct attack. His half nod was tolerant, almost affectionate.

"Do you mind?" he asked Peggy, cigar in hand.

She shook her head impatiently. And, after the briefest moment of hesitation, Tom Flanagan extended the silver case toward Duke.

"Sure. Why not?" Her brother slipped a cigar from the case, ripped off its end with his teeth, and jammed it into his mouth. "Dig me," he said. "I'm right in there with the big stuff, where the corn grows tall. Call me a cab and tell them to hold me a table up front. Our company beat the others by twenty gallons a minute last year, with one pump broke down. I'm just in town for a couple days, but I guess I can find my way around all right. Of course, I wouldn't go so far as to say I'd want to live here. It's a great place to visit, but—"

"Stop it, Duke," Peggy said. "You're not funny."

"I just growed up. Go upstairs and tell Mr. Rosenthal. Today I am a fountain pen." He grinned without humor. "Why don't we break out the liquor and make it a real old-time wake, fellas?"

"Tell me, Tom," Peggy said. "Whatever it is, I want to know it now."

He inspected the glowing tip of his cigar as though it were guilty of some offense, picked at an imaginary speak of lint on his conservatively striped trousers.

"Duke has managed to make it appear far more important than it is—or was. It doesn't matter now, and it was a mistake for me to have tried to keep it back, even briefly. The fact is, Mike was in a sort of jam. With the department, that is. I'm sure he'd have been cleared, but it looked bad."

"I don't understand. What kind of a jam? What looked bad?"

"He was under suspension, Peggy. There was a departmental investigation under way."

"Investigation—that's a nice way to say it," Duke said. "He was hit with a list of charges as long as your arm. Want to hear them? I've got them memorized! Failure to fulfill his duties as an officer. Collusion with persons engaged in criminal activities. Acceptance of a bribe. Foreknowledge of criminal acts and failure to attempt, by word or deed, to prevent same. Participation in said acts to the extent that they were observed and carried out with his full knowledge and accord. Negligence in regard to—"

"Duke," Tom Flanagan said, "I've told you once to shut up. I'm telling you again. There won't be a third time. Your father would have slapped your ears back long ago."

Duke puffed out his cheeks in a burlesque of pomposity, patted his stomach as he attempted a smoke ring.

"Big deal. All of a sudden I've got a new boss. Mr. Flanagan is running things now. But try, just try, slapping my ears back. You'd be surprised, buddy."

"Will you *stop* it!" Peggy exclaimed. "I don't know why you're acting like this, Duke, but I can't take any more of it."

"All right. Only I don't see why I should be expected to go along with all this double talk. He's dead. Okay. So is that any reason for not coming out with the truth? Mr. Flanagan here seems to think that's how things ought to be done—dragging it out and giving the facts to you a little bit at a time. But then, he's a politician, and I'm not. I'm just your brother, and Mike was only my old man, so I wouldn't know how to talk about it to you, not as well as a man who was there the night you were born and whose folks came over on the same boat and all. Me, I'm stupid and crude, and my way would be to give it to you straight from the shoulder, like this: There was a big book on Mike's beat—a hell of a big operation for a town this size. A real fancy drop behind a cigar store, with a chalk board and all, so you could sit around and almost believe you were in a broker's office, or maybe even in the stock exchange, instead of a place where you went to bet on the horses. And if you got tired of that, if the horses or the football games or whatever didn't go fast enough to suit you, there was a non-stop crap game and two tables of heavy poker working upstairs. Right so far, Mr. Flanagan?"

"I guess it will have to be told your way," the older man said. "Yes, what you've said up to now squares with what we know."

"And Mike was on the payroll. Maybe he was the go-between for somebody more important, somebody who was supposed to be able to give the place real protection. That hasn't come out yet. If that was it, he sure had lousy connections. Because they knocked the place off one afternoon. They knocked it off right after they picked him up in the cigar store, a squad from his own precinct house. A detective—one he didn't know—had been on his tail for two weeks and was in there looking at pipes when the guy behind the counter gave Mike the envelope. It had an even thousand dollars in it when they opened it down at the desk. And he couldn't explain it. I mean, he wouldn't. So he was suspended without pay, pending investigation, like it said in the newspapers. That was ten days ago, and last night, early, the neighbors heard a loud report, also like they say in the papers. And half on hour later the people downstairs found that their ceiling was—"

"But why didn't someone let me know!" Peggy exclaimed. "Ten days! You had plenty of time to write, Duke. You should have told me."

"He didn't want you to know. I guess he thought he could beat it and he didn't want you worrying for nothing. Or maybe he knew he couldn't beat it, and there was no use in spoiling your trip. Anyway, he told me not to mention any of it to you if I wrote. As soon as he got into the house that afternoon, even before I understood what it was all about and why he wasn't wearing his badge, he made me know that this was something you weren't to be in on."

Peggy turned to Tom Flanagan.

"You knew, too. And you didn't tell me."

"That's the way he wanted it, Peg. Maybe it was wrong. I can't pass judgment on that now. But that's how he wanted it, and I couldn't go against his wishes, not where they concerned the way he ran his life and his family."

She was thinking of the humiliation it must have been to that spirited man, being arrested in uniform by his own friends, the men with whom he strutted down the Avenue every seventeenth of March, white gloves immaculate, kangaroo shoes polished to a mirror gloss. Had they actually locked him up, kept him in one of those cells to which he had led, so often regretfully, so seldom with any real feeling of satisfaction, a never-ending procession of the unfortunate, the psychically ill, the criminal, the vicious?

"I just thought of another charge they could slap on him now," Duke said. "Two of them. Suicide's against the law isn't it? And how about jumping bail? You think you'll get your money back, Mr. Flanagan?"

The older man ignored him.

"You went his bond, then," Peggy said. "I guess I should have realized that. You've been an awfully good friend, Tom."

"Excuse me," Duke said. "It's getting pretty thick around here. I guess I'll sort of thin out."

He went down the hall to his own room, came back in a moment and swaggered to the outside door.

"See you," he said.

"Where are you going, Duke?" Peggy asked.

"Out. Just out. Is that all right, or do I have to get a signed slip from somebody?"

"I wasn't trying to keep you here. I just wondered. It would seem that tonight you might rather stay at home, that's all."

"Does it? Well, I don't. Or wouldn't rather, or however I ought to say it. So if there aren't any objections from you or Mr. Flanagan, I'll just leave quietly. Thanks for the cigar, Mr. Flanagan. I want to get down to the candy store and wave it around before it gets too short to be impressive. I'll tell all the guys to vote for you, if they get back from the Army alive and grow old enough to vote. Except, you don't bother with being elected any more, do you? You just get appointed to things, so you don't need anybody's vote."

"Will you be late? Do you have your key?" Peggy interrupted.

"I have a key. Don't worry about that, unless somebody changes the locks around here."

The door closed sharply behind him. A piece of glassware rattled on a shelf, and then there was silence.

"I'm sorry," Peggy said. "I've never seen him like this. It isn't like him. You know that."

"You shouldn't feel called upon to apologize. I can understand what he's going through. He doesn't know where to let out his anger against something which he feels is terribly wrong, so he strikes blindly, in all directions. He's a good, sound boy. It's just that he's confused at the moment, and he's very deeply hurt."

"But still, it's so unlike him. Tonight I've had a feeling almost as though he were a stranger. My own brother. He's so hostile. So hard and—yes, crude. Like one of these young hoodlums trying to be big-shots. That's not Duke's way."

"It won't last. He resents me because he thinks I've been too presumptive in handling things. Perhaps I was, but somebody had to take over, make decisions. You weren't here, there were no near relatives close by, and Duke was in such a state that I really didn't believe he should be left with the responsibilities that had to be faced. In his eyes, all this was an intrusion. But your father—your father was my friend, Peggy."

"I know. I'm grateful. Grateful for everything, and so will Duke be, when he's more himself. We're both upset in our own ways. Upset—that's a pretty weak word, isn't it? Hardly the one to express how I feel about everything that's happened, and what I've learned tonight. It was shocking enough to know that Mike was gone. To be told that he died disgraced, killed himself … Tom, I can't believe it. Somewhere, somehow, there's something wrong!"

Tom Flanagan pursed his lips and nodded with evident reluctance as he carefully flicked the ash of his cigar into a tray.

"I've had that feeling myself, Peggy. Mike Malone was the most honest man I've ever known. I can't understand how he could have gotten tied in with people like that. And yet the evidence all pointed to it."

"But what did he *say*? How did he defend himself when you talked about it?"

"We didn't talk about it. It was one of those cases where you don't ask about right or wrong. Mike was in trouble, and as soon as I heard about it I did what I could to help, as he would have helped me if matters had been reversed. He didn't want to discuss what had happened, and I didn't press the subject."

"Then he was guilty, is that it?"

"No. At least, I can't get myself to believe it. But the evidence was strong, and he never said a word to controvert it. I don't know why. I don't want to ask myself why."

"What of the others? The men who were running the gambling place? Did they implicate him?"

"They're professionals, Peggy. Men who coldly and deliberately choose to live outside the law and plan their operations and actions as carefully as any businessman. The risk of arrest is taken into account just as a department store considers the unavoidable risks in its own operation. When they are arrested they call for their lawyers and then clam up."

"Suppose they were afraid of what Mike might say? Isn't it possible that men like that could have decided he had to be—permanently silenced?"

"I don't think so. It's unlikely, because the stakes weren't high enough. I've talked to the D.A., and the best he expects of the case is to rap a couple of them with short jail terms. They wouldn't have committed murder under the circumstances."

Peggy left her chair and went to the windows which overlooked the street. In the yellowish glare of a lamppost part way up the block, a group of youths were clustered. They were too far away for her to know if Duke was among them.

"My father was no coward, Tom."

"No one could make that accusation. He had, let's see—six citations, I believe it was. And earned more. Twice, I remember, I felt he'd been overlooked, and I wanted to nudge a few elbows downtown. He wouldn't let me, any more than he would let me try to get him promotions I thought he deserved."

"He was no coward," Peggy repeated. "And I know that he was no crook. But we'll put that aside. If he had turned crooked, he wouldn't suddenly have turned yellow at the same time. He would still have stood up like a man to take his medicine when he was caught."

"I know what's on your mind. It's hard to answer it. But the revolver was in his hand—that presentation thirty-eight with the inscription. There were no fingerprints other than his. A damned thorough check-up was made. Even Duke was closely questioned."

She turned tiredly from the window.

"I don't know what to think, Tom. It's such a crazy mix-up. Look, though—they take photographs in a case like that, don't they? Before the body is moved?"

"Yes. They're on file somewhere. With Homicide, I suppose. Anyway, they'd be in the main photo morgue."

"I want to see them."

The shock on his face needed no words to convey its meaning.

"I know," she went on. "They aren't pretty. But I want to see them. I know how Mike lived, and it's my right to know how he died."

"Girl ... That's the worst thing you could possibly do to yourself! Don't you realize you'd have that picture of him in your mind for the rest of your life, every time you thought of him? It's wrong to hurt yourself like that, and it's pointless. Why in the world—?"

"But suppose they show something that would prove those gangsters really did have him killed? We don't know what information he may have had. Maybe they really were afraid of him, and knew that if they didn't shut him up something might come out which would send them to prison for a long stretch—or worse! Maybe to the chair! The evidence seems to say that Mike was crooked, that he was being paid off to protect a gambling joint. Why stop there? Why couldn't he have been mixed up with something a lot more dangerous?"

"Peggy, those photos have been studied by police experts. Thorough, painstaking men. If there were anything which the pictures could have revealed, they would have discovered it."

"I want to see them. You know how I should go about it?"

"All right," he sighed. "I'll help you. You know your own mind. And perhaps Duke is right. Maybe I do try to run things for others when I ought to be minding my own business."

"It isn't that way at all. I don't feel that way about any of it."

"I'll find out exactly where the pictures are, and if you still want to see them a few days from now, you can give me a ring. And while I'm on the subject of minding—or not minding—my own business, I got in touch with your mother's relatives. Her sister and an aunt should be here any time now, to stay the night. I felt that you should have someone with you, some women for company. If that was a mistake. I'm sorry."

"No, Tom. I'll be glad to have them here."

He looked at his watch.

"Maybe I ought to wait around until Duke gets back anyway. But let's try to put some of this out of our minds for the rest of the night."

"I'll make coffee," Peggy said. "I think we could use some coffee." And she went to the kitchen.

Three of her mother's relatives arrived before the coffee was ready. When Duke came home, well after midnight, he was staggering drunk.

CHAPTER FIVE
THE STINK OF MURDER

THE TWO WEEKS following the funeral passed with somewhat the unreal quality of a dream. There were papers and more papers to be signed and notarized, a vast tangle of legal red tape to be gotten through as her father's affairs were straightened out. Through it all, Tom Flanagan stood ready to advise, to point out legal shortcuts. He had, in fact, offered to act as executor, but that suggestion Peggy had turned down.

"In the end I'll have to take these things over anyway. I might just as well learn how now."

But it was more than that. Actually, she wanted no single detail to escape her attention, wanted nothing that might furnish a clue not to pass directly through her own hands.

She discovered little with which she had not long been familiar. A life-insurance policy for five thousand dollars, and war bonds with a face value of seven hundred. Deeds to two cheap lots upstate, together worth no more than three hundred dollars. A savings account of slightly over a thousand, a no-minimum checking account with a balance just under two hundred. In a safe-deposit vault, papers relating to these and to a small note he had co-signed for a friend. And that was about it.

She spoke of this to Tom.

"Where is it, the loot?" she asked bitterly. "If Mike was a crook, where are those neat bundles of crisp bills, the bonds waiting to have their coupons clipped, the black-velvet jewel pouches? Is this the estate of a man who was getting rich on graft? And that investigation—did they ever turn up a hidden bank account, another safe-deposit vault? There isn't a key which I don't recognize, a scrap of paper I haven't seen before. Where was he keeping his ill-gotten wealth—in the band of his hat? Well, I've even looked there, because he had a habit of keeping grocery lists and things like that in his hat when he was in uniform."

"They have their own explanation for that," Tom said. "They'd like to assume that he himself was gambling, and losing. Or that he was spending it on ... that he had a ..."

"That he was keeping a mistress?"

"Either one of those assumptions is ridiculous," he hurried on. "So they simply say that it might very well have been the first time he took a chance, that he got his feet stuck as soon as he stepped off the path. He was under surveillance, he was observed taking the pay-off, and he was arrested with the money in his possession. That's enough for them. Thank God I've got some influence around this town."

"What do you mean?"

"I'm going to bull through it. All the way. First they weren't going to allow a departmental funeral—"

"I didn't know that. It never occurred to me."

"Then on the matter of death benefits. There was talk to the effect that they shouldn't be paid, that only the money he had put in should be turned back to his estate. Because he was under suspension, you see, and there were some who had already tried him and found him guilty in their own minds. Well, I fixed that. Mike was never dismissed from the force. None of the charges against him was proved—or can ever be proved now. I've asked the District Attorney to keep Mike's name out of the trial against the bookies when it comes up next month, and he's agreed. The subject is irrelevant to his department's case. Next thing I'm going to do is demand that the suspension be withdrawn retroactive to a date precedent to his death. Damned if I won't get that thousand dollars back, too! There's no evidence that it wasn't rightfully his. It could have been a loan. It could have been anything."

Peggy smiled wanly.

"My father never had an extra thousand dollars floating around like that, Tom. Neither to lend nor to have borrowed. Let them hold it and put it in the Fund if nobody else claims it. It wasn't Mike's. It isn't mine, or Duke's."

"I guess you have a pretty low opinion of my methods, haven't you, Peggy? Influence, pull, knowing whom to see at the right time, doing a favor here and asking for two there—these aren't things that you believe in, or that Mike believed in. I'll never go down in the history books as a statesman, God knows. But some of the machinery of government is creaky. If a family on your block is starving, you don't wait for Washington to declare a national emergency and put them on relief along with eight million others. You pull a few strings and get the old man a job driving a city truck. Somebody has to drive them. And you've saved a man's self-respect, his right to walk into his house with his head up. You've saved a woman's right to send the kids down to the corner grocery without being afraid that this may be the time he'll turn them down. That's politics, yes. And who has been hurt?"

"There's no need for you to be apologetic with me. 'Politician' isn't necessarily a swear word in my dictionary."

He patted her on the shoulder.

"Let's keep it that way," he said.

Duke's reaction was different, and by it she saw how opposed their attitudes were growing.

"Great," he replied, when she told him of the condition of Mike's affairs. "So you haven't been able to find anything that would prove he was a crook. What does that mean? Where does that leave him, or you, or me?"

They were in his room, and he was knotting his tie—a flashy, hand-painted creation which featured a garish representation of a nude woman dancing in flame.

"Either way you want it," he said, "where did it get him? Maybe he was just a sucker. He still went up on charges, so where is the percentage? Or say he was really in, getting his where he could. If it was that way, who are you going to trust? All that came of it was that I got a rotten deal, and so did you, whether you want to look at it that way or not. Whether things ended up this way because he was stupid or bought isn't important. We've got to take the dirty end anyway. Only I'm not going to go on taking it. I didn't make this set-up, but I'm beginning to see how it works. And I'm going to get mine, and to hell with anything else. Me first, and let the other guy look out for himself."

It was hard to relate this harsh-voiced, quick-eyed person with the gentle little brother she had mothered as other girls mothered their dolls, reading him stories they both were young enough to almost believe, playing dress-up, keeping his nose wiped and bathing him until he grew old enough to be embarrassed. Now he was almost a stranger, with an alien way of seeing things, a hard swagger in his manner. And this was something which had happened almost overnight, for they had been together for several days before she left for France, when he came back from his mid-sophomore term at college and she was through with her teaching duties for the summer. He had still been her brother then, someone she recognized.

She watched him run a comb through his hair. He was letting it grow long in back, duck-tail fashion, and his sideburns were becoming exaggeratedly long. There was a type of girl, she knew, which considered this attractive, sporty, the mark of a classy date. And there must be girls; Duke was nineteen, healthy and alive.

"It's take or be taken," he finished. "That's the whole story."

"You don't really believe that," she said.

"Don't I? Wait and see. You won't catch me beating my brains out trying to scrape up a buck the hard way. Not when the stuff is lying around waiting for somebody to pick it up."

"Duke, that isn't the way things are. Sometimes it may look as though that were so, but eventually you find out that life only gives back what you put in. The way that looks easiest is the one that turns out to be the hardest, finally."

"You know who you sound like? Tom Flanagan. God damn if you don't. Him and his preaching. But how tough are things for him? A fancy house up on the Hill, and another one out in the country. Servants to open the door and pour the drinks, if you were ever invited to visit him. Look at the cars he drives, or has somebody drive him around in. And then show me the calluses on his hands."

"Tom Flanagan and your father," Peggy said heatedly, "started out on the same construction job together, working twelve hours a day carrying brick. When they were a lot younger than you, incidentally. Life took them in different directions, that's all."

"Yeah, I've heard all about it. Tom got interested in the union, and finally he was putting in full time on it and next thing he was in politics and Pop was pounding a beat and paying off for his uniform on the installment plan. And what happened after that? Flanagan got rich and Mike got a family to worry about. But they were still friends. Big deal. If they were such good friends, where was Flanagan when help was really needed, when Mother was first sick and some money would have given her a chance?"

"Mike didn't know how sick she was, Duke. And she knew how proud he was, and what it would have cost him to go with his hat in his hand, asking for charity."

"All right. But look how it ended up, that's all I've got to say. Nobody has to draw any pictures for me."

She was tired of that bickering conflict, and was glad to remember something to change the subject.

"There was a phone call for you earlier. Somebody named Woody. He didn't seem to hear me ask for the last name."

"Woody Russell. What did he want?"

"I don't know. When I asked if there was a message, he said he'd see you at the club."

"Okay. Thanks."

"What club did he mean?" she asked curiously. "I didn't know you belonged to any clubs outside of school."

"Just the club." He tossed the rebuff off as casually as he tossed a hairbrush into his drawer. She bridled under the sting.

"Listen," she said. "If you want me to take phone messages for you, you can afford to be a bit more courteous."

"It's just a club. A bunch of guys I know."

"That tells me a lot."

"For Christ's sake!" He slammed the bureau drawer so hard that the mirror above it rocked in protest. "Do I ask you to give me an accounting of everything you do? Can't you get used to the fact that I'm not a baby any longer? It's a social club, a place for the gang to get together without getting shagged off the street by some flatfoot on his way to clip an apple from the pushcart."

"A cellar club?"

"Yeah, I guess you'd call it that. Old man Gerfaldi calls it a basement apartment in the lease."

"That's quite a change from your fraternity at college, isn't it?"

"Dear old Kappa Rho Alphi Pi—strictly for the birdies. 'Fawtha wants me to entah the fi'm, y'know, but my int'rests lie along moah culchral lines …' Am I glad to be through with that!"

"You're dropping your frat?"

"I'm dropping college."

Somehow this was something she had been expecting. She took the news without a flicker of feeling; objection was automatic.

"Mike counted a great deal on you getting a degree. He sacrificed a lot of things to make it possible."

"Mike again! Mike! Every time I turn around it's Mike this or Mike that! I'm getting sick of hearing what Mike would have done, or what Mike would have wanted me to do! Is my whole life supposed to be made up of things he thought were important because he couldn't have them for himself? I'm tired of having my father's ambitions forced on me. I have a few ideas of my own, and sitting over a drafting board all day, letting some big-name architect pick my brains, isn't one of them!"

"Well, then, what do you intend to do?"

"I intend to mind my own business, for one thing. And that might be a good place for a few other people around here to start."

He shoved a wallet into one hip pocket, a fresh handkerchief into the other, and started to leave the room. At the door he seemed to remember something which had been buried in his anger, or which, perhaps, his anger had uncovered from something deeper.

"Just one thing," he said. "If this house is to be run by a man, let's get it straight. Let's get it straight and know who's who. In this house, now, it isn't Mike and it isn't Tom Flanagan. In this house it's Duke Malone, from now on."

It was a sweltering afternoon, a few days after that disturbing conversation, when she finally forced herself to go down to police headquarters. She had been putting off looking at the pictures of the scene that the officers had come upon when they forced the door, for she knew that they would be a hurtful shock, a dreadful memory always afterward. And it would probably be a fruitless effort to peer past the cloud of mystery into the truth. Yet she felt that it must be done, that every possible shred of evidence must be gathered and studied if her mind was ever to be at peace.

Heat slammed back from the streets and sidewalks in a shimmering glare. Men walked by with ties loosened, hats in hand, fanning burned, perspiring faces. In the doorways of stores and shops other men stood in shirtsleeves, blinking against the sunlight, glancing occasionally at the cloudless blue sky in search of some hint that the papers' predictions of two unrelieved weeks of scorching discomfort were in error. The tabloids featured the inevitable pictures of eggs being fried on the steps of City Hall, of bosomy young girls holding their skirts unnecessarily high as they waded the park pools. Editorials spoke of the "silly season" and anticipated the usual rash of miraculous wonders to be reported from the outlying districts. But people were growing sullen under that relentless baking; the cheery inanity, "Hot enough for you?" was being offered less often, was less banteringly received. Tonight the fire escapes of the slum sections would be crowded with mattresses in violation of all fire laws; additional patrols would be assigned to the city's parks, tacitly ignoring half a dozen ordinances while whole families set up temporary camps, gypsy fashion and in disregard of the privacy they usually guarded so jealously. It was in times like this, Peggy knew, that the index of violent crime rose sharply. Tempers were short, smouldering passions burst into flame at slight provocation. The dog days had always been a period of extra duty for Mike.

Crossing a side street, the asphalt paving gummily soft under foot, Peggy came across a group of children shrieking and splashing in the play of a hydrant someone had opened for them. Down the block she saw the foot patrolman carefully looking the other way; in good time he would appear upon the scene, all outraged authority, and turn it off, to the accompaniment of taunting jeers and suggestions that he might better employ himself in capturing criminals.

Suddenly she was remembering the children playing at the corner of her street in Paris, and then she was thinking of Jacques. All of that, for some reason, seemed to be a long time in the past. And Jacques had been almost forgotten, already, for he had scarcely been in her mind since he had left her at the airport. She had even forgotten to look for him, and wave as the plane moved lumberingly down the runway. He had been put aside as easily as a discarded textbook. There had been two letters from him, neither of which she had answered. The first had been almost formal in its expressions of regret for her father's death, and even its nostalgic references to their own relationship had been oddly stilted. The second still lay with a pile of mail unimportant enough to be neglected. It had not even been opened.

It must have been, then, she thought, some intuitive rejection which had kept her from giving herself easily to Jacques, which had protested so strongly and sternly when she tried to force herself into acceptance of his love. For, after all, if a woman does not bother to open the letter of a man who would be her lover, how could she open herself to him? Jacques had not been the right man to lead her to her completion as a woman. He had been charming and gentle and rich in tenderness. But somehow he had not been the man for her, the one to whom she must some day give herself with all of her being. Something she needed had been lacking in him, and in some part of her secret self she had known that, with a deep, ancient knowledge and sensing it, had turned away.

She climbed the twenty-seven steps leading to the entrance of the ugly building which, begun under one civic administration, had been completed after two others, with the result that the successive imposition of architectural styles had produced a monstrosity of sufficient notoriety to be cited in classrooms as an example of bad taste. Inside, she questioned the first uniformed guard she met and, after some confusion in the maze-like hallways, found the department for which she was looking.

The clerk was elderly and somewhat bemused, in the way of elderly alcoholics. His nose was bulbous and his head was egg-bald, and he stroked one or the other alternately as he talked. He had been advised in advance of her visit and its purpose; the photographs were at hand for her inspection. But—he looked worried—had she come alone, with no friend or relative?

"I don't know, Miss Malone. Them pictures, now, they're pretty gris—I mean, pretty strong stuff for anyone close to him to look at. I thought you'd have someone with you, it just seemed natural to expect that. It isn't that they're worse than most of them—some of the stuff we have here would turn your stomach. But when it's somebody you know, or somebody in the family ..."

"I'll be all right. I won't faint or have hysterics."

"Well, in this heat anybody could. It's on your say-so, then."

The photographs were in a large manila envelope with a string closure over which he fumbled for tantalizing moments. And even when he had them out he held them for several seconds more before turning them over to her.

"Young Charlie Barnes took these," he said with professional appreciation. "Always tell Charlie's work, the way he sets it up, the way he uses his lights. Something like Alexander Alland's style, say fifteen years ago. Taught Charlie myself, before my legs gave out so I couldn't lug that weight around all the time."

She managed to get them away from him before he began the string of rambling reminiscences which were bubbling up in his mind, and took them to a table near the room's high windows. Steeling herself against the impact of personal emotion, she drew up a chair and turned the first photograph face upward, like a gambler studying a hand of poker ...

In the unnatural, strange-smelling chill of an air-conditioned drugstore, she made the phone call to Tom Flanagan. He was at first incredulous of her request, thought she was joking. Then, realizing that she was serious, his manner changed to one of puzzled concern.

"But why, Peggy? Why should you want to get on the force? A girl with your training a policewoman?"

"You mean I'm too smart to be a cop?"

"I don't mean that at all, and you know it. What's the matter with you, anyway? There are plenty of college graduates taking the exams these days, which is a hell of a good sign, and the way things ought to be. The tradition of the dumb flat-foot has had too long a run, and wasn't true to begin with. What I'm saying is that you have spent several years in preparing for a career as an educator. Aside from the question of intellectual waste, I don't feel that a background like that qualifies you for the practicalities of the job you're talking about. Familiarity with Goethe's poetry isn't of much help when you have a hopped-up mugger on your hands."

"Tom, I am asking you for a favor. I've never asked anything from you before this. Everything you've done for me—for us—has been unsolicited, and it's been appreciated. If you don't want to do this, I won't be offended and I won't be less grateful for the help you've already given. But I want a badge, and it seemed to me that you were the right person to go to, the man who could cut through channels so that I wouldn't be held up."

"Why do you want that badge, Peggy? Have you asked yourself?"

She hesitated. There were questions which she could not now answer completely, questions which must be, to some extent, evaded.

"Let's just say that I'm trying to vindicate my father. Is that enough?"

That was true, if ambiguous. If to Tom it seemed to mean that she had some romantic notion about carrying on for her father, of clearing his name by the way she conducted herself, she would not bother to contradict him. But her reasons were deeper, more direct than that, and involved far more practical problems. And she couldn't reveal them to anyone, not even Tom. At least, not yet.

"There *is* an opening, isn't there? Didn't I recently read that the number of policewomen was going to be increased?" she prodded.

His deep sigh was like that of a parent who knows that some childish project will end in failure, yet realizes that it cannot be forbidden.

"All right, Peg. If it's what you really want, we'll get you in. Call me in the morning. If there isn't an opening, we'll make one."

She hung up, feeling that at last she was in a position where she stood a chance, even if it were slight, of accomplishing her purpose. For she had decided, even before she left headquarters, that she knew the general direction in which the answer to Mike's death lay. If she could go back along the way circumstances had but recently taken him, meet the same faces, place herself in the same situations, she might be able to find the key to the evil that had been done.

Because Mike had been murdered.

She knew that now, and knew it certainly, although she could never have proved it. And the evidence lay in the police photographs, of which she had expected so little.

It wasn't anything which the police had been careless about or had overlooked. It was something the implications of which probably no one but she could have been expected to understand.

Mike had been slumped in the chair, his head lolling far to the left and forward. His left arm had rested naturally on the chair's arm, limp-wristed and relaxed. His right arm hung over the chair on that side, the revolver in his hand held dangling by the forefinger crooked about the trigger.

It had taken her a moment to realize what was wrong. Then she suddenly knew that her father had not killed himself. He hadn't killed himself because he couldn't have. Not that way.

Mike couldn't have fired that revolver, because for over a year his index finger had been stiff and useless, immobilized in a slightly curled position after he had broken it in subduing a wife-beating drunk. For some reason he hadn't wanted anyone to know—and wasn't there something strange about that, too? But Peggy had noticed the way he held a fork, the way be used a pen, and she had even seen him, when he did not know she was watching, fingering the trigger of his thirty-eight—with his second finger. She had never mentioned it, because he was so evidently trying to conceal it, and she was apparently the only one who was aware of it.

It was little enough to go on. But it was enough for Peggy, enough to convince her that Big Mike Malone had not died by his own hand, enough to force her decision to join the force and try to uncover ...

Uncover what? She didn't know what. But something. Something which would shout that Mike was what she knew him to be—a simple, honest man, trying in his own way to make the world a little more decent a place to be in.

She couldn't tell anyone, because she suddenly trusted no one. That initial, intuitive sense of wrongness had grown to a conviction that there was a deep-rooted rottenness in the circumstances surrounding Mike's death. The more she thought about it, the more certain she became that her feelings were not misleading her. Mike's passing had been most peculiar.

It smelled of a frame.

It stank of murder.

CHAPTER SIX
FIRST LESSONS

WITH TOM FLANAGAN smoothing the path for her, in addition to the fact that certain regulations were being overlooked in the city administration's anxiety to strengthen its quota of policewomen, Peggy found herself being sworn in on her new job in far less time than she had dared to hope for. The written examinations on basic law, civic administration and the like, she passed easily. She had no trouble with the tests in calisthenics, swimming, life-saving, or first aid. The physical requirements seemed surprisingly low, although she saw several other women flunk out on them—a three-foot, six-inch high jump, a twenty-pound abdominal press, a forty-five pound weight lift to snatch and clear. Tumbling gave her some trouble at first, and she was never good at judo: she knew the theory, and what must be done to turn another's attack into defensive advantage, but she could not generate much enthusiasm for tossing another person around. Each time she was obliged to dump her instructor on his head, she felt she ought to apologize and offer her sympathies. On the pistol range she had no trouble in qualifying; the metal cut-outs that popped up and moved jerkily in their erratic patterns were obviously make-believe, even with their painted faces. Some of them, like the one whimsically created in the image of Hitler, were old friends, remembered from the days when Mike had brought her here to learn the use of firearms.

Technically, she should have remained a probationary officer for a period of six months. What actually happened was that she asked for assignment to the detective bureau immediately, and the request was granted. She paid six dollars for her shield—gold, and similar to a lieutenant's badge, instead of the silver shield worn by most male officers—and received it at the same time that she was issued her own revolver, took the oath, and signed the record book. On that same day she was assigned a temporary working partner, Detective John Fanson, and was sent out with him on park patrol.

She knew at once that her partner didn't care for the detail. He thought of it, in fact, as a sort of punitive assignment, vaguely connected with an altercation he had had with a superior over the handling of a recent case, and that might well have been so. By it he was reduced, in a manner of speaking, to the rank of beat pounder in plain clothes, for the duties entailed nothing more specific than general observance for the purpose of preventing crime or disorder. Also, it made him the butt of a great deal of none-too-subtle kidding from other members of the force. Speculation as to whether his underclothing consisted, in part, of lace-edged panties was typical of what he must put up with so long as he was teamed with a woman, and along with this was combined a variety of earthy suggestions as to how he might best introduce the rookie to a proper understanding of her duties. Policewomen were still regarded with chauvanistic amusement by a large part of the force; there were men who would never be able to accept them as equals in the world of law enforcement, or even as having any rightful place there.

But John Fanson was a conscientious man, and whether or not he enjoyed an assignment had little to do with how he carried it out. He set about teaching her the things that they had neglected to mention at the Police Academy, and at the same time tried to bolster her confidence in her ability to handle the job she had taken on. Yet all the while, she was sure, he must be taking coldly analytical notes for the report he would have to make on her. Alertness ... observance ...

Like most rookies, she was overly observant, too much aware of petty detail. To her mind, ordinances were being shattered right and left as they strolled through the park in the general direction of their first call station. Walks were being littered, unleashed animals committed nuisances, the anti-noise law was flouted. When she drew these facts to Detective Fanson's attention, he smiled briefly.

"You're right. Exactly right. You could make a pinch on everything you've mentioned, and maybe make them stick. In fact, you could probably arrest everybody in this park including me, and find some law to justify it. If all the laws in this country—any country—were observed to the letter, everything would come to a dead stop. But so long as the paper litter isn't more than the sanitation department can handle easily, so that it isn't an eyesore that spoils the looks of things, there won't be any drive on people who drop gum wrappers. How you are going to work is going to be up to you; my own method is to leave people alone so long as they are acting in a way which seems logical and reasonable.

"Take that man, the fat one, who is about to drop what's left of his leaky ice cream cone. It's beginning to drip on his hands and on his clothes. He can't put it in a trash can, because there aren't enough in the park and we haven't seen one for a quarter of a mile. So he drops it, and in ten minutes the pigeons will finish it off. Or take that puppy over there, chasing butterflies. Granted, no one should try to raise a dog in the city, but a lot of folks do— because they're lonely, because they can't raise children—for all sorts of reasons. Me, I feel that anything unfortunate enough to live a dog's life in this town ought to be allowed a little leeway, at least when it's still just a few days from its mother and isn't even big enough to bite its own fleas. And as for those teen-agers back there who were making such a hell of a racket—so long as they make noise I don't worry about them. It's when they slip by without a sound that I begin to wonder. The right to make a noise ought to be written into the Bill of Rights, instead of discouraged. If more people made a noise about what's on their minds, we'd know a hell of a lot more about what ought to be done to keep the ball rolling in the right direction."

"I wasn't suggesting that we should have done something about any of those things," Peggy said, feeling that he misunderstood her, and must believe her to be very stupid indeed. "What I was wondering about was, how far do you go? Suppose you're after one thing and you run into something else? How far do you go in ignoring one crime because you're after something bigger?"

"If you're driving a fire truck to the school house, you don't stop to wet down a burning garbage heap, do you? Or, if you're on your way to a routine check of the dump, and you pass a house with smoke coming out of the windows, what does common sense tell you to do? In some instances, though, you might have direct orders to ignore anything but the dump fire. Maybe somebody called in and said that there were enough cases of T.N.T. down there to blow the town up. It's something that you use your best judgment on, and pray that you're right when you make up your mind. I passed up a street brawl once because I was tailing a man who was pushing drugs, and I thought he was going to lead me to the big connection that day. I could have dropped him and broken it up, but I stayed with him instead, figuring that the prowl car would be along any minute. All he did was go home and go to bed, and I found out later that his big connection had left the country a week before. And two men were knifed in that brawl, and both of them died."

His mouth twitched in a sour grin, and he said, "You pays your money and you takes your choice, and the chances are that you'll get hell from somebody either way. Now, did you notice that since we turned off at the statue of that mean-looking cuss back there—"

"Dante?"

"Yeah. All hope abandon, and all like that. Anyway, we passed two guys sleeping on benches, both of them pretty evidently having been lushing it. Any comment?"

"They didn't seem to be bothering anyone. One of them was dressed better than the other. The second one looked like a panhandler."

"All right. Now, I know both of them. The one who looks like a panhandler is just that. He's too far gone in alcohol and his own misery to be rehabilitated, not with the money and facilities Social Service works on now. Jail won't help him, and neither will a stretch in the psych section. He's been in both more times than he can ever remember. He's asleep now, and that's the best thing that can happen to him or that he can do for himself. It wouldn't do anybody any good if a cop came along now and shook him awake and sent him stumbling somewhere else. Follow me?"

"Yes, of course."

They paused at a fountain, and he held the faucet open for her while she bent to drink. They might have been co-workers on lunch hour from a nearby office building, a young married couple on a holiday, lovers snatching a few moments together. She wondered what people thought of them as they passed. Did anyone suspect them of being police? Her purse swung with conspicuous heaviness; a light summer dress, such as the heat demanded, left no other place for the unfamiliar burden of a revolver.

"The other fellow," John Fanson said as they continued on their way, "is a house painter who lives around here. A family man with three kids. Been down on his luck lately, and can't find regular work. Gets a couple hours here, half a day there. It isn't enough, and he worries about it, and he does his best worrying in bars. It's just about enough for that, and he's really beginning to slip. And none of this is any of our business."

He detoured around a king-sized baby carriage with twins on proud display by a middle-aged, rather astonished-looking woman, then found her again.

"But I'm stingy. I pay taxes too, and I object to having another dipso on the city's hands, and another family on the relief rolls. Three kids! That's a lot of milk for me to help buy. So, when we go past the merry-go-round, I will stop to speak to Officer Brown. Officer Brown will be there, because he is supposed to be there at this time of day, and also there are a lot of young mothers with their children, riding the wooden horses. Officer Brown," he said with a perfectly straight face, "is very fond of children."

"You're kidding me, now."

"Yep. But not much. They told me you were just back from France, so I had to try talking like a French novel."

"What about Brown?"

'He knows what things are about. If we just walked by, he'd look right through us, never blink an eye. No uniformed cop who knows his business will ever recognize a detective until he's sure it's all right. After we've spoken to him, though, he'll take a stroll back along the way we came. He won't bother the panhandler. He'll raise hell with the house painter, though. Maybe threaten to charge him with loitering, vagrancy, and public drunkenness. The painter will talk about his civic rights, argue a while, and finally decide that making an issue of it isn't worth the trouble. He'll leave the park damning all cops and the system. He'll go home, where the whole neighborhood, including his kids' friends, and maybe somebody who might have a job for him next week, won't have a chance to see him sleeping on a bench. And he'll be out of the way of some rum-dumb bar acquaintance who floats by with a plan for promoting a bottle somewhere."

"But he isn't a vagrant, really," Peggy objected. "And if you stood outside any bar you could just pick up drunks as they walked out."

"Right. So let's suppose he has a little money in his pocket. He looks as though he ought to have. So he's flopping there, dead to the world. What an easy score for some kid who needs just one shove, either way, to go straight or crooked, to decide whether he's headed for the big house or, for all we know, the governor's mansion! Maybe by getting the man out of sight we've saved more than just what was in his wallet. It's like taking the keys when you leave your car."

"And Brown does the dirty work?"

"Yeah, he's the villain. A plainclothesman doesn't advertise if he can help it. And besides, I know that guy back there. I'd rather not shag him. We were in the army together. He was my sergeant for a while."

The whistle of a peanut stand attracted him. He stopped to buy a bag, offered them, and when she declined, walked along scattering the shucks as he shelled them.

"Well, let's see if we can find Brown. Everybody knows that there's never a cop around when he's needed, when he could do some good. And then you'd better make your call-in. They're probably wondering back at headquarters whether you've captured any criminals yet, Officer Malone."

CHAPTER SEVEN
LADY COP

THEY made no arrests that day, nor the next. On the third day they were moved to shoplifting detail and sent out to check department stores.

"Dime stores are hot," Fanson told Peggy as they left a store where they had loitered and window-shopped for half an hour. "You noticed how, in the last few years, you can't get waited on in a ten-cent store, how you have to look around for somebody to take your money and wrap up whatever it is you're trying to buy? I guess maybe some efficiency expert has it all figured out for them—how much they stand to lose by theft if they cut the staff by twenty percent, and how that balances out against the wages they save. Anyway, they're wide open, most of them, and the section managers can't be expected to see everything. Counters are neglected because it's cheaper to do it that way then to keep enough clerks in the place. I'll make you a bet that we could walk into the next five-and-dime and come out with our pockets loaded.

"Now maybe that seems unimportant. Who's going to bother, you say, to take a chance on the kind of stuff you can pick up in one of those places? I'll tell you who. Kids. Maybe a boy sees a pack of stamps he'd like to add to his collection, or a girl notices a lipstick. Something like that. So they pick it up and walk out with it. And they've had their first go at petty pilfering.

It's an easy way to start. Somebody is being socially irresponsible, because it's profitable. They'd probably be indignant if you tried to tell them so, and put the blame on the kids' parents, home life and all that. But I never knew of a crook who deliberately went out and made his own opportunity, not at first. The opportunity to steal was already there waiting for him, and it looked easier than staying honest."

There were several points in what he said which Peggy felt were open to question, but she never got around to mentioning them. For, as they turned a corner, they came upon a scene the violence of which immediately filled her with panicky fright.

In the center of a small, but growing crowd, a shirt-sleeved youth was trapped. His clothes were bloodied and torn; his face was marked by the blows of a dozen fists. Unsteady on his feet, he rocked his head from side to side from the shoulders, an injured animal at bay. His eyes ferreted here and there, seeking the escape which did not exist. Ringed about, he feinted first in one direction and then another, thrusting for some weakness in the pack that snapped and snarled like hounds harassing a fox. Even as Peggy stopped, paralyzed with dread, one man reached out and grabbed him by the hair. A second, emboldened by example, drove his fat, flabby knuckles against the youth's unprotected neck.

"Kill the son of a bitch!" Peggy heard a high-pitched male voice cry from somewhere in the rear of the crowd. An approving growl murmured from several throats. Peggy turned to John Fanson, but he seemed to have forgotten her presence. He was studying the situation, quickly, but without excitement. She tugged at the sleeve of a man who was on the periphery of the circle and was trying to elbow his way in.

"What happened?" she asked. "What's the trouble?"

"How the hell should I know?" he said. And then, shoving a woman to one side, he shouted, "Let me at that bastard! Kill that son of a bitch!"

"Someone ought to call the police," observed a man who was carrying a briefcase and who looked rather like a bank clerk. He pursed his lips and peered uncertainly about him. Obviously, he meant someone else.

The woman who had been elbowed back had caught Peggy's question, and she was eager to display her superior knowledge of the matter.

"It's a purse-snatcher, honey," she said. "He grabbed a girl's pocketbook, right out in broad daylight, and she screamed and he ran and they caught him. I saw the whole thing, right from the beginning. Right out in broad daylight, mind you! Why, a body can't even walk down the streets nowadays! I tell you, it's a crying shame the way the police allow these things to go on, and taxes going up all the time too. What are we paying for, that's what I'd like to know, when you aren't safe anywhere …"

"All right, make way there," Detective Fanson spoke up, his voice ringing with authority over the snarling excitement of the crowd. "Police coming through. Break it up."

He shouldered into the ring, and Peggy fought to follow close behind him. The youth had been knocked down by now, and two men were kicking him, while others jostled closer, eager to take their places.

"Police, damn it!" Fanson snapped at a beefy man who was obstinately refusing to move from what he considered an excellent vantage point. "Move when I tell you to!" He slammed past roughly, and spun one of the kicking men off balance, stepped in front of the other.

"I'll take over now, boys," he said. "Just move back now, give us some room."

He flashed his badge, staring hard at one of the men who had taken a threatening step toward him.

"Isn't it horrible?" a shining-faced woman exclaimed excitedly. "Just too, too horrible!"

The expression in her eyes did not appear to be that generally understood to indicate horror, however.

"What is it?" some newcomer demanded of anyone who would listen.

Half a dozen explanations were offered.

"Some guy throwing a fit ..."

"Molesting a girl, they say. I guess he was exposin' himself ..."

"... a fight. That fellow lying there, and two others."

"They ought to take care of those sex maniacs, that's what I say. You know what I mean. Just like an animal; that's all that can cure them. Either that or keep them locked up, out of harm's way ..."

"That must be the girl standing there with the cop. See him blowing his mouth off and showing his badge all over the place when he finally got here? Wonder how she feels, with everybody looking at her and knowing about it? What the fellow tried, I mean ..."

Fanson bent over the youth, who was feebly writhing, only semi-conscious, on the sidewalk.

"We'll be needing an ambulance here," he told Peggy. "You can call in from the drugstore—that's closer than the box. Somebody may have phoned for the prowl boys already, but they wouldn't have thought of an ambulance." He raised his voice to the crowd again. "Everything's taken care of, folks. Just move along now, you can't be of any help here."

Some took a reluctant step or two backward; most of those watching stood their ground, with a defiant stubbornness.

"He's letting the girl go, you see that? He's keeping the fellow, but he's letting the girl go ..."

"What's happened? What's the show, bud?"

"... plainclothes detective. He caught this guy running away ..."

"... ran out of some store, right into the detective's arms. The question is, who caught who?"

"Have to be desperate to try to rob a store in broad daylight. Some poor, hungry bastard out of work, I suppose ..."

"... beat the hell out of him."

"... stealing a loaf of bread, or something. The cop beat him up."

"Didn't she hand him something just now? You see that? What ..."

"... gave him something out of her purse, and he let her go."

"Look at that poor guy lying there! Too handy with his black-jack, if you ask me ..."

"... pay them off and you never have to worry ..."

"The cop beat him up ..."

Two or three people detached themselves from the main body of the crowd and started to trail along after Peggy, as she hurried toward the drugstore; then, after some hesitation, they melted back to the more promising attraction.

The single booth in the drugstore was occupied. Without pausing, she strode to the partition which marked the pharmacy, opened her purse and displayed the wallet to which her shield was pinned. It was her first test of its authority, but she did not even think of that.

"Your private telephone, please. Official business."

The clerk seemed startled, but did not question her request. He stood by curiously as she made the call, and afterward followed her to the door; until then, news of the excitement down the block had not penetrated the place.

White-faced, Peggy pushed her way back to Fanson. The mob had grown in her absence; at its outskirts, understanding of the situation was fantastically garbled.

"Shot the kid, they say. Just a kid, but he put a bullet in his back ..."

"They hand out a badge to anybody with pull, these days ..."

"... that wasn't enough, he had to drag him across the sidewalk, rough him up some more."

"... standing there, letting the poor kid bleed to death ..."

There was ugly threat in the voices. The undertone of mutterings was accented by an occasional cat-call directed at the detective. The atmosphere was thick with the threat of more violence to come.

John Fanson had moved back to the brick wall of the building, and the youth, moaning, lay at his feet. Fanson had one hand on his hip, drawing his suit jacket back far enough so that his badge, as well as a glimpse of his shoulder holster, was evident. No longer attempting to break up the crowd, he was simply waiting with an air of stolid determination.

"What do you want me to do?" she asked. "Should I try to make them move on?"

"They won't move now until they see a blue uniform with brass buttons. It won't do to try to force it. They'd just get stirred up more. We'll wait. Seen the girl around?"

"No, I—just a minute."

She had caught sight of the woman to whom she had first spoken, the one who had claimed to have seen the whole affair. But, when Peggy questioned her now, she seemed to have lost her memory.

"I'm sure I don't know what you're talking about. I don't want to be mixed up in any of this."

"But you said that he snatched a girl's purse. If you could point her out, I'd like to talk to her. We can't get the full story without her, don't you see?"

"I'm not mixed up in any of all this. I didn't see anything and I don't know anything. I don't want to have anything to do with it."

"You don't have to. You could be a valuable witness, but that's not what I'm asking. I'm looking for the girl."

"Well, if there was any girl I guess she'd be looking for you if she wanted to be found. I don't know anything about it. And you can't make me say any different!"

"… policewoman," rippled through the crowd. "… the other one's mixed up in it some way … going to arrest her …"

Defeated, Peggy went back to Fanson.

"Skipped out, has she?" he said. "That happens more often than not. So there won't be any case, and there isn't even any charge to book him on, except maybe obstructing traffic and causing a crowd to collect."

She wondered how he could joke, even grimly, at such a time. She was truly afraid of the temper of the mob of which they were now the center. And where *was* the prowl car? Maybe is wasn't so funny, that joke about never being able to find a cop when you wanted one.

John Fanson evidently guessed what was going on in her mind, for he grinned reassuringly.

"Don't expect too much of people, ever. And don't be surprised when things like this happen to you. It's a hot day. But you needn't worry about it getting any worse. It won't. We haven't got a race deal on our hands. If the boy happened to be a Negro, and we were on Melville Street, or if we were in the shore side and he—"

"Why dincha pick on somebody ye size, flatfoot?" someone yelled.

"... lousy grafters, all of them ..."

"... shoot you as soon as spit on you ..."

"You can't really do much for him here," Fanson's voice came back to her "His ribs have been smashed in, and I think his left wrist is broken. But it would give them something else to think about if you went into the first-aid act."

Peggy knelt beside the boy, took a tissue and began wiping the bright, light bubbles of blood from his nostrils. He was just about the same age as her brother, she thought. His hair had been trained to that same duck-tail style.

She was still kneeling over him when she heard the first wail of the sirens, the clang of the ambulance ....

"It's a real hot day," Detective John Fanson said to her, later.

CHAPTER EIGHT
BROTHER PUNK

D UKE was becoming a problem.

A fatuous way of expressing it, Peggy thought, even as the phrase entered her mind. Hardly adequate to describe the complex personality change which seemed to be taking place.

More and more, his time was being taken up with activities which, vaguely explained as they were, apparently centered around the cellar gang and its neighborhood haunts. He took to getting up at a progressively later hour, and it was often well into the small hours of morning when Peggy heard him letting himself into the flat. There were even occasional nights when he did not come home at all, and these absences he pointedly did not explain. He knew that his conduct was a matter of concern to her, and seemed to take a sardonic pleasure in making oblique references to it, half taunting, as though challenging her to voice disapproval.

"Meeting of the Boy Bird Watchers of the Twelfth Ward, tonight," he might tell her as he was leaving. "I'm on the cookie committee."

She gave up trying to make meals for him; oftener than not he disappeared in the middle of their preparation, or refused to eat them because he had just eaten, or was about to eat, the offering of some diner or hamburg stand in the neighborhood. The telephone would ring as she was setting out the table service;

after a few minutes' low-voiced, cryptic conversation he would retire to his room for those important rites of hair brushing and necktie selection, then suddenly be gone, leaving her to stare across the steaming plates at an empty chair.

He had no job, and made no effort to get one, yet he did not lack pocket money. Rarely, he might ask her for a small loan, and these sums he always repaid. She had offered to make some financial arrangement so that, either out of her salary or the money left by Mike, he would have a regular weekly allowance, but this he refused.

"I'll make out," he told her. "When I'm hurting, I'll tell you."

"But where are you getting your money, Duke? You aren't working. I don't see where it comes from."

"I make fudge and sell it. And sometimes I get a chance to do a little fancy crocheting and tatting for the people up on the Hill."

With one exception, his friends never came to the house, nor, apparently, did he go to theirs. The exception was Woody Russell, and Peggy's immediate reaction was antagonistic.

Woody was no adolescent. He was a man who might have been in his late twenties or early thirties but he maintained, or tried to maintain, the air and attitudes of someone much younger. His language was salted with the latest catch-words common to the bobby-sox set. He was flashy and slangy and quick. About his presence there was an aura of superficiality and guarded falseness, hinting at areas of secrecy, of slyness.

He was not the sort of person, Peggy thought, to whom Duke would previously have been attracted. Duke was by no means stupid; he knew what Woody's type represented, and what it represented was nothing of any importance or worth. He might not have voiced disapproval; he would simply have ignored someone like Woody out of sheer disinterest. Yet now he was giving a large part of his time to this new association. They sat in the kitchen and brewed coffee, or they talked over a can or two of beer, and always their conversation had to do with matters which involved the problems of "finding a live one" or "making a score." Situations were either "crazy" or "a drag, man," girls were "gone chicks" or "flipped beasts," and they would go on talking in this shallow, short-hand jargon for hours. Late into the night she would hear the murmur of their voices; in the morning the coffee cups or beer cans were waiting for her to take care of when she awoke.

After the first time or two that Woody came to the house, Peggy scarcely tried to be polite, but he did not appear to notice. Or, if he did notice, he did not care. Stopping in to see Duke, and not finding him at home, he would toss his jacket aside and relax on the couch with a magazine while he waited. Giving Peggy scarcely more attention than he might have given a maid, or cleaning woman, he browsed about the apartment with almost insolent freedom; neither the refrigerator nor Mike's books were inviolate, and she came to resent his manner and presence more and more as she was subjected to them. At the same time, she hesitated to make an issue of Duke's friendship with him, for this was Duke's home as well as hers, and it was certainly his privilege to bring into it whomever he chose. She could only wish that he had chosen someone else.

What conversation there was between them was carried on almost entirely in monosyllables. The bell would ring, and there he would be, leaning back against the banister as though he had been forced to wait for an unconscionable period.

"Duke in?"

"No."

"Okay if I wait?"

"I guess so."

At such times he looked at her without appearing to really see her. Yet a few minutes later, as she moved about the room on some task of house-cleaning, she would experience a feeling that she was being covertly watched. Turning, she would sometimes be in time to catch the flicker of Woody's eyes as they twitched away from her. She was always extremely self-conscious in his presence; two or three times she dreamed of him, but when she awoke she could not remember what the dream had been. It was always just out of grasp, and all she retained was a sense of restless discomfort.

Duke and Woody obviously shared a vast amusement at her new job. To her face, Woody went no further than to grin slyly at some reference Duke might make, but she was sure that it was the subject of several of those secretive conversations. Duke, on the other hand, made no effort to conceal an attitude which was close to contempt.

"You don't learn so good, do you," he said to her one day. "I'd think the police force would be the last thing in the world you'd tie in on now."

She couldn't tell him her reasons. There was no possibility of confiding in him now. And, preoccupied as she had been with trying to learn her job and become oriented to it, she had really done nothing in the direction of learning more about Mike's death. She knew no more now, several weeks after having joined the force, than she had when she first studied those police photographs. She was beginning to know her way around the department, but that was all. Doubt of ever accomplishing more was creeping into her mind, and she became defensively angry.

"Someone's got to have a job around here!" she snapped back. "If Mike isn't here to pay the rent, it looks as though it has to be me!"

He looked startled, then grinned.

"Play it cool on the gold issue," he said. "I'll get up my end of it."

"Yes? When? How?"

"Pretty soon, now. And don't worry how. Woody and I have a little production warming up. We'll make."

"Robbing gas stations? That sounds like his style."

"Don't come on square. Who asks for a rap? This is legit, through and through."

And that was all he would say about the matter then. Whatever the nature of this dubious enterprise, however, Peggy soon noticed that its preparation did not appear to require either regularity of hours or much work. Day after day, on the way to or from her shift, she would pass Duke lolling in front of a candy store with some of his gang, or she would notice him moving about in the murky interior of the pool hall. Woody was seldom with him at those times, but on the few occasions that he was Woody always appeared to be the center of the group and to be treated with a kind of boisterous deference.

The fact that she was a policewoman was no secret, and Duke's own attitude evidently set the key for the gang's antics when she passed by. It became a game with them to try to annoy her. As a teacher she had become well acquainted with the tactics of adolescents bent on such a purpose, but then she had always been in a position to defend herself with some form of discipline. Here she could do nothing, and Duke seemed to enjoy her discomfiture as much as the rest.

"Can't you quiet down that bunch of yours?" she finally asked him. "It doesn't make my job any easier, having a pack of young punks cat-calling after me on the street."

"Well, you're the cop of the family," he shrugged. "If they're breaking the law, you know how to call the wagon."

CHAPTER NINE
THE FLESH IS WILLING

S HE called Tom Flanagan instead. She had seen him less frequently lately, although they had twice lunched together, and he seemed glad to hear her voice.

"I was just thinking of you," he said. "Been meaning to phone for days, but I've been a little self-conscious about intruding since—since you returned from France." Then, when he heard that she wanted to talk to him about her brother, "Why don't we have dinner together?" he suggested. "Maybe a roadhouse later, if you don't mind being seen with a man who's old enough to be—twice your age. It seems to me you deserve a bit of relaxation for a change."

So it was arranged, and that evening he picked her up at the flat and they drove ten miles out the Indian Parkway to an inn where the food and service were as near perfect as any she had found in Paris. Duke had not been at home when she left, and for that she was glad. Not because she did not want him to know that she was dining with Tom, but because she did not trust herself to remain calm if Duke was again rude to her father's old-time friend.

Whatever the cause of Duke's dislike, it was obviously not mutual. When the conversation turned to her brother, Peggy noticed that Tom spoke of him without rancor, and sometimes in a manner that was almost paternally affectionate.

"There are times," he said at one point, "when I deeply regret never having married. Aside from the loss of a woman's companionship, I am being more and more forced to see that I have deprived myself of things which become increasingly important as one grows older. I might have had a son like Duke."

He sat musingly twirling his wine glass for a moment, then grinned.

"Next week, *East Lynne*," he said. "No one can be more pompously pathetic than an elderly politician."

In her mind Peggy had been hearing the ghost of an echo: "A son like Duke—or a daughter like you," and she wondered if the thought had been in his mind also. He *could* have been her father, youthful though his appearance was, and in many ways he was constantly reminding her of Mike.

"You're not old, Tom. It's not too late for you to marry and raise a family, if that's what you really want."

"I don't know, Peg. Do people just coldly decide to get married and then look around for someone to put the proposition to? I couldn't. And, to be biologically frank, the woman would have to be considerably younger than I, for a number of reasons. At my age one doesn't know too many marriageable young ladies— and fewer still who would be interested."

There had been a time, Peggy had been told, when Tom Flanagan and her father had both courted the girl who was later to be her mother. Mike had won out, eventually, and they had all three remained friends afterward, even made jokes about it. But it was strange to be sitting across the table from the man who had once been your father's amiable rival, being aware of him as a man, and thinking of how differently all their lives might have turned out. You, of course, would never have been born, and it was somewhat uncomfortable to consider that. Never, that is, unless—

But you couldn't think that way about your mother. Nor about any of the three of them. She was sure that in her mother's life there had never been any such episode such as, for instance, her own experience with Jacques. "Courted"—that word from a bygone day and bygone attitudes—described exactly what had passed between her mother and Tom Flanagan. Still that suggestive thought intruded: Tom Flanagan *could* have been her father ...

Annoyed with herself for the line her thought had taken, she was relieved as Tom's words called her back to the original subject of their discussion.

"... growing pains," he was saying. "Just have to let this phase run its course. Once he gets back to college, he'll forget the cellar gang in a week."

"But that's just it! He isn't going back to school."

"Are you in financial trouble?" Tom quickly asked. "If it's a question of—"

"Money doesn't enter into it. He says he's not going back, and he's as much as said that he has no intention of getting a regular job. My own feeling is that Woody's influence is back of a lot of it."

Tom thought this over, his frown as much one of puzzlement as concentration.

"It's difficult to imagine anyone having that much influence over the boy. What do you know about this Russell fellow, anyway? Describe him."

"He's thirty, give or take a couple of years. Five feet ten, weighs maybe one-seventy. Brownish eyes, when you can get a look at them. Handsome, I guess. Clothes good, but loud. A sharpie type, with nothing, really, to distinguish him from the rest of the species. No visible means of support, but I've seen him driving a Cadillac. Close-mouthed when he's around me. From what I've gathered, he's recently come up from New Orleans."

"And he and Duke are going into some sort of business. No idea of what that might be?"

"None, except that it seems to involve the whole gang that Duke hangs out with. I can tell you one thing, though—it won't be anything as innocent as selling Christmas cards to win a bicycle."

"It doesn't sound too good," Tom admitted. "A cellar club mixed up with a man such as you describe could be a lot of things—all spelling trouble. They might be planning to take small bets from school kids. Nickel and dime stuff. Or—Peggy, would you recognize the smell of marijuana?"

"That's one thing that's out. I—well, Duke may be mixed-up in a lot of ways, but he's not vicious."

She could not bring herself to tell Tom that, with the same thought in mind, she had not only made a systematic search of ashtrays but had gone through her brother's personal belongings.

"Then we'll just have to wait and see what develops. It wouldn't do any good to have this Russell picked up until we have more of a line on him. If the police couldn't pin anything on him, he'd just be more of a big shot to the kids. I'll put in a word downtown to have the gang watched a little closer, if you want me to, but that might scare the man off, and I'd like to see what he's up to. Frankly, I think the best strategy at present is for you just to continue to find out what you can. If it turns out to be something serious, I'm sure we can pull the boys out before they get into too deep water."

He reached across the table and patted her hand, holding it strongly in his for a moment.

"And now, Peggy, it's time to stop worrying and think of something pleasant for a while. When we've finished our coffee, if you don't mind driving a few miles further up the river, I know a place where the liquor isn't cut too much and where the music isn't entirely given over to jitterbugging. Could you be interested?"

"I think," Peggy said, "that that is exactly what I feel like doing this evening."

When she thought about it later, Peggy was struck with the similarity of the early part of that evening to a day she had spent in the company of her father—an event marking a birthday when she was too old for children's parties but too young to ignore the occasion entirely. Only then dinner had been a meal in a cafeteria, followed by a walk in the park, and a double malted in a soda shop had taken the place of the roadhouse. There, however, the parallel ended, for on the trip homeward Tom Flanagan had begun to show an interest in her which was anything but fatherly.

There was a full moon, and as they drove back down the turnpike it had ridden along with them, reflected shimmeringly in the twisting river. For a time its beauty had been lost while they sped through a deep, raw cut in the hills. Then, as they came into the clear again, Peggy gasped at the sheer impact of loveliness which was revealed. Through the scudding mist of clouds which habitually lay at the top of Smoke Mountain, the satellite rode in cold, proud brilliance, while, far below, the waters flung back a glittering jewel of distortions.

Tom slowed, then drew off the road onto a clearing. He shut off the motor, and they sat there in silence while Peggy drank in that splendid radiance. Finally Tom began to speak quietly, pointing out to her the locations of the craters Tycho and Copernicus, then going on to find various of the planets and constellations.

"I didn't realize you were such an astronomer," she said. "Where did you learn all this?"

"I have had a little observatory set up at my place. It isn't much, but it helps me pass the time. And I am a very lonely man sometimes, Peggy. Very lonely."

He had taken her hand. He began to fondle it with a gentle pressure. She pressed back understandingly. Surely she could understand what it meant to be lonely, now. Briefly, she thought of Jacques, wondering if he too were lonely. She rather thought not; Jacques was not one for whom loneliness was intended, and there would be some other girl by now ...

She did not object when Tom put his arm around her, nor when he drew her head down on his shoulder and kissed her temple. Instead, she snuggled up to him, wanting him to understand that she knew, and shared, his need for affection, warmth against the chill gloom of isolation. It was later that what she felt, and perhaps what he felt, changed and became something else, with a more physical meaning.

They had been sitting quietly together in that fashion for some time before Tom began to become restless—and that same restlessness seemed to be strangely communicated to Peggy as soon as she sensed it. He fiddled with the radio, turned it off. Finally the hand that held hers brought her fingers to his lips, then dropped to the slenderness of her waist, drawing her body to his. She half turned to meet him, was crushed tightly to him as their mouths joined. Astonishment vied with passion for possession of her senses. She had not expected anything like this of him—nor of herself. Yet she found herself responding. Her back arched with a quick surge of pleasure to the strong, grasping clutch of his hand on the fullness of her hips, and a soft call of excitement bubbled in her throat. He was almost hurting her, holding her that way, but that didn't matter. If anything, there was a kind of pleasure in it.

The suddenness with which their mood had changed from near-platonic affection to demanding passion was almost explosive, as though pent-up emotions had been building up pressures to the bursting point for a long time, and without their knowledge. When Tom fumbled at the bodice buttons of her dress, she raised her shoulders eagerly to help. They ached to be taken, those hard-nippled breasts which he was laying bare, just as her whole body ached with longing and anticipation, as all her senses ached with hunger to be dominated and possessed. A glance downward at her twisting thighs, gleaming palely in the moonlight where Tom had rumpled up her skirt, excited her even more. Her own nakedness to his touch sent tingling thrills along her spine, and she drew one leg upward in order to rub her skin raspingly against the roughness of his clothing.

He looked down at her as she lay so, her eyes shining and hot, her clothing disarrayed, body tossing with anxious need, a tumbled, tousled creature his for the taking. He wantoned her breasts, and little moans of delight replied. He touched her knee lightly, and her thighs moved loosely to his direction, willing and wanting to please.

Now he took her hand again and placed it upon his own body, waiting for the moment when her excitement should take over as guide. Her fingertips touched, hesitated ...

"No! No, Tom!"

She flung back from him, frantic and panting.

"What ...?"

"We mustn't! It's wrong! There's something wrong! I don't know what it is—don't ask me, because I can't explain. It's just that something gets in the way, and it's like smashing into a stone wall!"

Her voice rose close to the pitch of hysteria before she caught control of herself, and even then she was shaking so that she could barely manage the buttons of her disarranged clothing.

"Will you take me home, Tom, and—and try to forgive me."

When the car drew up before her building, Peggy already had her hand on the door-handle.

"Would you like to come up for a minute? A night-cap?"

"No. No, thank you. Not tonight." He stared out at the street and then he said, "I'm sorry. I didn't mean to have anything like that happen between us. You're the finest girl I know, Peggy. I guess I just ... Let's try to forget it, shall we?"

On impulse she reached out with that same sympathy which had precipitated the whole episode, and stroked his hand.

"It wasn't your fault any more than mine. After all, we'd been dancing and drinking and—we just fell into the trap, that's all."

She got out of the car and closed the door.

CHAPTER TEN
SHOPLIFTERS

AFTER WORKING for several days with John Fanson, Peggy had been teamed up with Ada Granados, and from then on she usually worked with one or the other alternately. It was while she was on shoplift detail with Fanson that she made the first arrest on her own. And that came about because while John was off talking shop with one of the store's private detectives she had noticed a woman browsing about the various departments in a loosely cut spring coat. True, the store was air-conditioned, but the outside temperature was well into the nineties.

"Places like this," Fanson had told her, "have their own staff of privates, but we keep an eye out anyway. One thing they have to handle for themselves is theft by their own clerks, either by short-changing or ringing false sales. That domestic-looking woman at the curtain counter is Madge Harper, a professional spotter hired by a merchants' association to shop their stores and watch for irregularities in the way the sale is handled. You'd be surprised at the number of people who put aside their consciences when they're working for a large corporation, and the schemes they devise to tap the till."

And later he had pointed out another woman, a woman with blue-gray hair and the haughty manner of wealth.

"A rich klepto," he said. "Husband's a big surgeon. Maybe you ought to watch her work, just for practice. Only we don't try to pick her up, because that would make everybody mad at us. She's a good customer, in her own way, because her husband has a deal with the store. They watch for her, and when she comes in they mark down everything she takes. Then they bill her husband, with a good slice added for anything they may have overlooked."

They saw the woman pick up two or three small articles before she left, and at each counter where she paused a store detective stopped immediately afterward, spoke to the clerk, and made a notation in a book.

"She isn't very clever," Peggy observed.

"No, just wealthy." And they had gone on.

But the woman in the coat didn't look wealthy. The coat was in need of a cleaning, and the heels of her shoes were heavily worn to the side. Her hair needed attention, and she had a run in one stocking. Hovering around the jewelry department, she kept throwing quick, bird-like glances over her shoulder even while her nervous fingers pretended to examine some item or other. At last she fumbled furtively with her sleeve, then turned and walked away. Peggy looked for John Fanson and, not seeing him, followed.

There was one clerk at the photo supply section, and there were three customers, to one of whom he was demonstrating an expensive movie camera. The woman hardly hesitated now. From a display on the glass counter she picked up a cheap Brownie and slipped it under her coat. Then she made for the store's entrance. There was nothing for Peggy to do but go after her alone, hoping with all her heart that her partner would suddenly appear. He didn't.

You had to wait until they were outside the store before you could make an arrest. Before that point you couldn't prove intent—they could say that they couldn't get the clerk's attention and were looking for someone to wait on them; they could say that they were so used to self-service supermarkets that they forgot they were in a department store; they could say that they had stepped from the counter to ask the opinion of a friend, or to examine the object in better light. But it was logically assumed that none of these explanations were valid once they had left the premises. So Peggy waited until the woman was on the street and hurrying up the block toward a subway entrance. Then she overtook her and briskly tapped the thin shoulder.

"Haven't you forgotten something?"

The woman gave a violent start and turned frightened, washed-out eyes on Peggy. Then, seeing that it was not the uniformed figure she dreaded, a momentary relief cleared her features, leaving only suspicion.

"I think you've made a mistake, miss."

"No," Peggy said. "I think you have."

Doubt again crept into the woman's eyes.

"You must have mistaken me for somebody else. I don't know you. I haven't time to be bothered now."

"Would you mind showing me what you have stuffed up your sleeve? I know about the camera under your coat."

The woman's jaw fell. Then she made an attempt to draw herself up in an attitude of indignation. She shrugged her arm from Peggy's grasp.

"Who do you think you are, bothering me like this? I think the heat must have got you. Go away now, before—before I call an officer."

"I am an officer," Peggy said. "And you are under arrest. Let's take a quiet walk back to the store, now. If there's any explanation to be made, you can make it there."

She felt anything but secure. She wanted John Fanson's assured presence to back her up. But she tried to appear cool and

authoritative. Locking her arm firmly through the other woman's, she turned back to the department-store entrance.

And then the woman began to plead. She had three children
at home, she said. Her husband had abandoned them. There was
nothing to eat in the house. The things she had stolen—they
weren't things that she would have wanted for herself. What in
the world could she possibly do with a camera, except sell or pawn
it? The piece of costume jewelry she had taken—it was the sort
of thing that a young girl might have been interested in, nothing
that she, a grown woman, could use. She would turn them over
now, and Peggy could see that they got back to the store.

"Three little kids," she begged. "Sweet little kids who don't
know what's happened to them, or why Daddy went away, or why
they didn't have any breakfast this morning … They're waiting
there now for me … I promised I'd bring something home to eat.
Please! Please!"

"I'm sorry," Peggy said. "We'll see what can be done about it."

"… playing a game when I left. 'Supper,' they called it, and it
was all about what I would bring when I came back. Hot dogs,
that was what they hoped for. Hot dogs, and maybe canned
peaches afterward. Good God, lady, don't you know what it is to
be poor? Don't you know the difference between somebody like
me and one of these big-shot racketeers you see riding around
like they was kings? Please …"

"I … You'll just have to come along now. Don't worry about
the children. They'll be taken care of."

"Will you promise me that? Because they're all alone,
waiting …"

"I'll see to it myself. But I have to take you in. That's my job."

"Then I don't think much of your job. Maybe a smart young
girl like you could be figuring out how to help people when they
get troubles like I've got, instead of waiting to catch them doing

something wrong. All I was trying to do was feed my kids, not get anything for myself. *Please,* lady!"

Peggy could not answer, for a hard ball of nausea had begun to form in her throat. She shook her head.

And then a thick-faced man had fallen into step with them. He flipped his lapel just enough for Peggy to see the special badge pinned inside.

"City?" he asked.

"Yes."

"I couldn't quite make you. I was watching you both back there in the store, and I didn't know if you were on her or working with her. When you both came out, I didn't know which one to pick up first."

"You mean, you were thinking of arresting *me*?" Peggy asked.

He looked mildly surprised.

"Sure," he said. "Why not?"

The woman's story was true. Peggy and John Fanson established that by going to the two-room cold water flat she and the children occupied. There were two boys, one eight and one five, and a girl of six, all of them thin and too small for their ages.

As part of their game the children had clumsily set the rickety card table which served for their meals. The two younger ones were merely curious and disappointed that it was two strangers and not their mother at the door. Later they were excited by the prospect of going for a ride somewhere to have dinner and spend the night with some other children. But by the older boy's questions, Peggy soon realized that he sensed what was happening, that he knew his mother was in some sort of trouble with the police, and that he was hiding this knowledge from the others. He tried to appear as innocently entranced as they at the prospect of their unexpected adventure, but Peggy saw his chin tremble as he helped his smaller brother straighten the torn lining of his cap in preparation for the journey.

The two women from Social Service were cheerful and reassuring when they arrived in response to the phone call Peggy made from a neighbor's flat, and they agreed with the little girl that her broken-nosed doll should certainly come along too. One of them was already telling a story when they left, and the smaller boy was laughing when he turned at the door to wave at Peggy.

"And this," Peggy said to her partner when they were alone in the flat, "is the place we're supposed to search for stolen goods."

She looked at the cracked and mismatched dishes on the table, the bureau with part of an orange crate supporting one broken leg.

"You search," she said. "You find the incriminating evidence. I'm going to bawl."

She sat down on a chair that wobbled dangerously, put her face in her hands and began to weep. Detective John Fanson cleared his throat and went to a window, where he became greatly interested in the pigeons on the next roof.

"One thing you learn in this business, sooner or later, and one way or another," said Ada Granados, "is not to listen to the sob stories. They may be true, or they may not. You just have to grow deaf when they start."

They were sitting over coffee in a cafeteria located in an old part of the city once known for the number of artists and working craftsmen who lived there, but now mainly given over to eccentrics of one type or another who believed that some sort of bizarre exhibitionism was a quite satisfactory substitute for talent. These stereotyped oddities were a permanent part of the place, and to it they brought little but a dreary viciousness. The incidence of overt perversion was high enough among them to have forced the cafeteria's management to do away with wash-rooms in an effort to avoid scandal. It was known that drugs sometimes changed hands at the place, and it was for evidence of this that Peggy and her partner were checking. Acting on a stool-pigeon's tip, they had been dropping into the cafeteria each after-noon to observe the actions of a plump little man who habitually occupied a table there for half an hour or so each day. So far they had nothing.

Ada nibbled at the bit of Danish pastry she was leisurely con-suming. She scowled as a mannishly dressed woman passed by with an openly inviting smile, and then continued with what she had been saying.

"But probably the most important thing to remember is not to go in on a job alone unless it's something you're absolutely certain you can handle. There are situations that a woman simply can't cope with, and she's a fool if she tries to. You didn't know Nora Vancey—she got hers before you were around. You'd have liked her. She was a nice kid. But that was just the trouble—she was a kid, in some ways. She wanted to grandstand."

"What happened to her?"

"Everything. Everything except murder, and it came close to that. She stumbled onto something by accident, and she handled the job wrong all the way down the line. Some guy she met in a bar one night when she'd been on the force a couple of months turned out to be pushing the queer stuff. She went out pub-crawling with him and a couple she knew, and after a while she noticed that he kept breaking ten-dollar bills. So right away she got big ideas about taking a counterfeiting ring all by herself. She went to work with the heavy romance, and he asked her for another date. And that led to another one, and so on. All this without making a report. For all headquarters knew about it, she might just as well have been what she told him she was—a bookkeeper. Do you want part of this? I should watch my weight."

Peggy shook her head and Ada continued:

"Well, eventually she got around to letting him know she was on to his racket and that she thought he was a pretty clever boy to make an easy living like that. Also, she told him that she knew some people who might like to buy a large slice of queer if the price was right. That seemed to interest him, and she went on working it until, she thought, he was falling right into her hands. What she didn't know was that he had been into her purse and found her badge and I.D. card.

"That man's money wasn't the only thing about him that was queer. He had to be insane to take the sort of revenge he did. He stole a car one night and drove her out to an abandoned quarry and went to work on her. He beat her up and then he raped her and then he beat her up again. It went on that way, and when he wasn't able to rape her he thought up a few other things to make her do, and to do to her. He'd take his belt and whip her into doing some unspeakable filthy thing, and when she'd done it he'd whip her for doing it. When he couldn't think of anything else, he made her grovel in mud and eat filth.

"It didn't do her any good to beg. He liked to listen to it, but it just made him wilder. Finally she became unconscious, and she was unconscious next morning when they found her. And she had almost bled to death, because before he left he—oh, well, never mind. You get the idea."

Sickened, Peggy shuddered violently. Such brutalities seemed unbelievable. Yet just that sort of thing formed a large part of the crime news one read every day. It happened in all stratas of society, burst out of the most unlikely types of individuals. The mild-looking man who sat beside one on the subway might be riding toward a scene of the most shocking depravity; the kind-faced woman across the way could be the one whom the papers would next day headline as the murderer of her own children.

She had often heard it expressed that one had to be a hypocritical sadist to want to be a cop. And there were times when the job seemed cruel. She was beginning to understand some of what Mike must have gone through, for Mike had not been a cruel man. And, gradually, she was beginning to understand that her job was not merely one of protecting society against criminals, but of saving sick individuals from themselves.

"When you think of some of the things that people do to each other," she said, "it's enough to make you ready to check out of the human race."

"I've seen my share." Ada nodded. "More than my share. And I don't mean just on this job, either. I knew more of that kind of stuff when I was fifteen than most people learn in a lifetime."

It was a curiously unfinished remark, and although Peggy wondered what was behind it, some intuition told her not to ask questions. Ada lighted a cigarette, seemingly lost in thought. Twice she was about to say something, and twice she changed her mind. The third time she went ahead.

"You asked me about my father, once. Was he a cop, and all that. I guess I might as well tell you—there's a good chance that you'd find out some other way eventually, and you ought to have it straight.

"My old man," she said, "was a dip—and a four-time loser. When he went up for the big stretch, I was just finishing grammar school. My mother—well, it didn't take me long to catch on to that. I slept in the room next to the one in which she ... entertained."

"I'm sorry," Peggy said, dropping her eyes from Ada's. "I didn't mean—"

"You were interested enough to ask, weren't you?" Ada said harshly. "Well, listen, then. I went to high school knowing that my father was a crook and my mother a drunken whore. Where did that leave me? What sort of chance did a kid like that have?"

She picked at the table edge with a thumbnail, and her voice crept into the past, remembering.

"You know where I could have ended up—where I should have ended up, by all the rules. And I almost did. Sure, I stole penny candy from the corner store. I stole bottles of milk from doorsteps, and strings of bagels that the bakery truck used to leave on the delicatessen doorknob early in the morning. And once a butcher gave me fifty cents and two pounds of soup meat to go down the cellar with him. Get that—two pounds of soup meat. That's how hungry I got sometimes, when my old lady was too drunk to do business."

"Our man is leaving. I suppose we might as well—"

"No, let me finish. I'm not ashamed of it, because it all happened to somebody else, a long time ago.

"I joined a gang—a mixed gang. Coeducational, in your language. Some education! None of us were out of our teens, but ... Anyway, there was a point where I balked. Maybe because of my mother and what I'd seen in my own home, if you could call that a home. I wouldn't go along with the sex stuff. When the parties got rough, I walked out on them. I I didn't know that wasn't my privilege."

She looked for an ashtray, couldn't find one, and flicked ashes onto the edge of her saucer. There was a lengthy pause before she continued.

"There was one boy I liked a lot. He was tough and he was smart, and his name was Shadow. He was next in line to head the gang if Nickie couldn't duck the draft. I was flattered when he began paying particular attention to me, and when he asked me to go to the club alone with him one night, I scarcely hesitated, even though I knew—or thought I knew—what he had in mind."

Her mouth had tightened to a thin red streak. The pain of remembered hurt, Peggy wondered? Rejection of what she had been? Some inner thought of vengeance? It could have been any or all of those. Ada took a long drag at her cigarette and let the smoke dribble in rolling waves from her nostrils.

"The clubroom was in the cellar of a condemned loft building, and there was no one there, just as Shadow had promised. And I was right about what Shadow expected—but not about what was going to happen afterward. What happened was that all the fellows, except one or two who were chicken about a deal like that, walked in. How many of them? I try not to remember that. It was daylight when they let me go home."

"You mean … ?"

"I mean they put the boots to me," Ada said bluntly. "Call it a gang job or whatever you want. And Shadow came back for a second helping."

"I'm—sorry," Peggy said.

"You mean you're shocked. You can't understand how a woman can tell such a story about herself. Well, I can't either. Maybe I ought to go to a head-shrinker for the answer to that. But I do know one thing—that night provided the shock I needed to jolt me out of the way I was drifting. I left home and got a job and went to school at night. Those next few years weren't easy, and there were a lot of times I almost gave up. But I made it in the clear.

"If you have to feel sorry for someone, maybe you can feel sorry for the ones who didn't break with the gang. I hate them too much to feel sorry about what's happened to most of them by now—and what's waiting for them. I hate the creeps and the crooks and the whole rotten bunch, and every time I've gone soft I've had reason to regret it afterward. I guess a social worker wouldn't think much of my reasons for taking that City exam a couple of years ago, but that's how it is. That's why I'm a cop."

She glanced at her wristwatch and, after a last draw on her cigarette, snubbed out the butt. In silence the two girls left the place.

CHAPTER ELEVEN
FALL GUY

AFTER WHAT HAD HAPPENED at their last meeting, Peggy was far from anxious to call Tom Flanagan again. But she needed his advice, needed to talk to him as she and her father had once discussed her problems. Because something had to be done about Duke. She had learned something more about the "business" he had entered with Woody, and she was afraid that he was heading for serious trouble. She made the phone call.

"Peggy," Tom said, when she had sketched in her problem, "would you consider having dinner at my home this time? Maybe without so many distractions we can get more done in the way of constructive thinking than we did last time."

"Yes, of course." The "of course" was necessary, so that he shouldn't think she held that other evening's incident against him.

"Then I'll stop by for you at the same time?"

"No. No, don't come to the house, please. I don't want to give Duke a chance to start any more unpleasantness. I'll meet you in front of the Patchin Building. Same time."

She arrived early for her appointment, and she spent the extra few minutes nervously pacing in front of the building, her mind fuming at Duke. As much as anything else, she resented the time he was costing her—time she felt she should be using in trying to clear her father's name. With her mind so much taken up with

the problem he presented, she was unable to think clearly or con-
secutively on that other matter. Time was slipping away; she had
a feeling that every day which passed made it just so much harder
for anything to be accomplished in that direction. And yet she
could not simply let Duke go his way. Her responsibility to the
living was certainly as great as any responsibility to the dead.

The trial of the men who ran the bookie joint had finally
resulted in one being convicted and given a short jail term. He
didn't seem to be much worried about it, and Peggy asked John
Fanson to give her a line on him.

"Small time," he told her. "Never more than a two-bit stoolie,
too scared to really go into business and face up against the big
boys. Funny how he should turn up now in an operation like
that. Real funny."

Peggy thought so too. A bought fall-guy, with Mike the real
problem to be gotten out of the way—that was how she read it.
Supposing—just supposing—there was something really rotten
in the force and Mike had found out about it. And then suppose
again, since you'd gone that far, that the people involved had discovered that he was onto them. They hire a cheap goat to take a
rap, and set him up in business on Mike's beat. When he finds it
and makes his report, they ...

They what? She couldn't follow that line any farther. And how
high in the upper brass would you have to be to pull a frame like
that? How far up did the rot extend? Chief Nixon? Commissioner
Lyons?

And then, if all your suppositions had been correct, what had
Mike found out? What sort of racketeering or graft was involved?

She had been surprised to learn, during her first few days with
John Fanson, that there were illegal enterprises of various kinds
which were operating with the full knowledge of the police, and
her first thought was that this was what Mike had discovered.

For example, there was a pawn shop which was known to receive stolen goods; there were bars which remained open after hours, speakeasy style. Or take that warehouse reeking with the pungent odor of fermenting mash as they passed.

"We don't bother about that," Fanson told her, seeing her nose wrinkle at that obvious evidence of an illegal still when they walked by.

"Oh? And when do they pay us off?" she had asked indignantly.

"They don't," he grinned. "It's just that it belongs to the Federal men, and they've decided it's not quite ripe for picking yet."

In each such case, it seemed, there was some good reason for not taking action yet. It did not mean protection. At lease, not necessarily ...

Prompt to the minute, Tom Flanagan drew up to the curb in his conservative black Packard.

"Waiting long?" he asked as he helped her in.

"If I were, it wouldn't have been your fault. You're on the dot."

"I was afraid I'd be late," he said as they swung out into the flow of evening traffic. "I had to take a big army wheel around the water works and then out to the airfield, so that meant using the limousine. But I'll be damned if I can stand riding around behind some fellow in a monkey suit when I don't have to, and I try not to inflict it on my friends, so I took a chance and went home first."

Peggy slid down luxuriously in the big seat.

"This will do," she said. "It's good enough to go for the mail in, anyway."

"I didn't mean to sound ostentatious. Do I do that often?"

"No. You never sound that way. That's why it's funny. Something that seems so perfectly natural to you is so far from the way I've lived that it's slightly fantastic to me."

"What's this about Duke?"

"Let's save it to go with the coffee. I'd rather not be any more upset before dinner."

Tom's home was a large, white Georgian structure, built from plans drawn mainly by himself. Set well back from the street and approached by a sweeping drive, its landscaped grounds took in half of the entire block, their boundaries marked by a row of tall hedge trees. A butler met them at the door, and was immediately dispatched to mix Martinis, while Tom led Peggy to a sofa before a vast, stone fireplace, the uncovered chimney of which rose two full stories to the ceiling, a balcony along one wall marking the normal levels of the other rooms. Tom watched her eyeing the ceiling, and smiled.

"When I was a boy," he said, "we once lived in a house where the ceilings were so low that even my mother had to stoop to go through the doorways, and she was not a large woman. I promised myself then that some day I was going to own a house with a room high enough to fly a kite in. I almost made it."

"I was just thinking that it must be quite a job to keep the cobwebs down."

"I believe the housekeeper sends up pigeons, or something like that."

Over cocktails they discussed Peggy's job, for the most part. She had half-a-dozen amusing stories to tell about herself and the blunders she had made, and Tom was sympathetically interested. He asked questions about the officers she had met, and seemed to have a personal acquaintanceship with everyone she knew, even down to such details as the maiden names of wives and the ages of children.

"So you're going to stick with it, are you?" he asked. "Well, if you like it, that's fine, but I didn't think it was for you."

"I don't like everything about it. Nobody could. But I've got another reason for wanting to stay on now. Duke—"

"With the coffee ... remember?"

"Dinner is served, sir," said the butler.

CHAPTER TWELVE
KID STUFF

THEY ate in an alcove apart from the formal dining room, at a small table next to a picture window overlooking a part of the city and one of the older, smaller reservoirs. It was a leisurely meal, and they finished it by candlelight. Looking down over the water, Peggy remarked at one point, "I didn't know there was so much good living to be had out of piping water to the city's dishpans, Tom. Do you get a bonus for Saturday nights?"

"There isn't," he chuckled. "I hope you don't think I make enough money as Water Commissioner to have built a house like this! But I do make friends, and it's my friends who built this house. For instance, a few years ago there was a rule that no city contract would be given an out-of-state firm. That made it very cozy for some people, and it cost the city money. Then, when the Deerhead Reservoir was being planned, a group of men from another state came to see me. They wanted a chance to bid, and they had figures on similar work they had done which plainly showed that they could probably save the city about ten percent. On a reservoir job, that's not peanuts. So I started to fight the restrictive ruling, and finally the papers got interested and we won out. Sure enough, their bid was low. The work was finished on time and satisfactorily, and the taxpayers got a break for a change."

Peggy looked puzzled.

"I don't see—"

"How that helped me? It didn't, directly. But sometime later one of those men had advance information of a stock transaction which could be turned into money. He let me in on it, and I made thirty thousand dollars in one week. And all of this, I want to stress, was legal and legitimate. The only people who lost anything were the contractors who had been gouging the city for years because they thought they had things all sewed up."

They returned to the living room for their coffee, and with it Tom ordered brandy.

"You may leave the decanter," he told the butler as they were being served at the cocktail table before the fireplace. "And then I shan't need you any more tonight."

"Yes, sir." The butler withdrew—there was no other word for that discreet departure—and Tom spent a few minutes working over an elaborate panel of knobs and dials until he found a program of concert music on the radio. From concealed speakers at several points in the room the familiar romanticism of Shubert's "Unfinished," softly enveloped them.

"And now," Tom said as he seated himself in one of the facing chairs which flanked the couch, "let's talk about Duke. What's he up to this time?"

"I think he's up to his neck in a mean little shake down," Peggy replied. "Maybe it's more than that. I'll tell you what I know, and you decide."

She hadn't wanted the brandy—the Martinis had been very dry, and the dinner wine excellent, so that she had already drunk enough to be aware of that odd sense of displacement which warned of slight intoxication. But it was already poured, and it complemented the coffee to perfection. She tasted it in humming-bird sips as she told Tom the story.

"First of all," she said, "I've got to tell you that what I know I got through a stool-pigeon. Even at the level these kids are working on, there are informers. This one is called Billy-the-Mush, and he's—well not effeminate, exactly. Weak sister. Eager-beaver style. Too anxious to please everybody, so you have a feeling he'd do anything to please anybody. Do you know what I mean?"

"I know the type," Tom nodded over his coffee. "They're not pleasant at any age, but they seem to become more offensive as they grow older. They start out with a grudge against themselves, and it shows as a grudge against the world—or whatever their small worlds encompass."

"Except that they don't dare stand up against the world. They lick its boots, even while they hate it. Tattletales at ten, turncoats at thirty."

She touched her tongue to the brandy and let a drop or two trickle down her throat. The warm night breeze stirred the curtains at the French windows leading out to the terrace. Somehow she felt that Tom and she were in exact sympathy, that whatever she said would be precisely understood, in all its implications.

"But I didn't come here to talk about Billy-the-Mush. Whatever he, or people like him, may be trying to buy doesn't interest me. You know the old watch-your-car-mister racket? As soon as you parked, some kid would show up and offer to keep an eye on your automobile for a quarter or half a dollar—payment in advance. If you didn't come across, no telling what you'd find when you got back. Maybe the hub caps would be gone, maybe the tires would be slashed or the body scratched up."

"I remember, but I thought it had died out."

"This is a switch. Woody and Duke have set the kids up with buckets and sponges, and they're supposed to be washing cars. For a dollar they wipe the windshield and headlights and sort of wave the sponge in the general direction of the rest of the car.

There's no ordinance in this town against washing cars on the street. I looked it up."

"And they injure the car if they're refused?"

"Billy says no. There's a switch there, too. Nine times out of ten, nothing happens. About every tenth time the driver comes back and finds his car gone. No, not every tenth time. Say one car out of every couple of blocks they work. That's enough to spread the word through the neighborhood."

"They're *stealing* cars?"

"They're certainly taking them without the owners' permission. Billy-the-Mush says the cars are just driven to another part of town and abandoned. From the complaints that have been coming into the precincts, that appears to be true. A call comes in that a car is missing. Maybe it's found two blocks away, within half an hour. Maybe it's towed in for illegal parking next day; they like to leave them in front of hydrants, in restricted zones, and so on."

"The cars aren't stripped or anything like that?"

"No. Quoting Billy again, Woody says that's kid stuff. What he wants is for word to get around that it's a good idea to have your car washed when one of his teams shows up. He's told them that they'll have the whole town sewed up in no time, that every one of them who is out there now with a bucket will be driving around bossing another crew in a little while."

"I'll be damned," Tom said. "The way you explain it, it doesn't sound as though it could possibly work as a shakedown, but they seem to be putting it over." He refilled her empty glass and asked, "Do you know how they work, exactly?"

"Pretty well, if Billy wasn't singing off key. Woody bought an old sedan that Duke drives. They use that when they take the kids out and spot them around. They put them out in pairs, and Duke keeps driving around, moving them, seeing that they have fresh water if they can't find a gas station near by, and so on. Woody and he meet at specified times and they cruise in Woody's car with two or three other kids that have been hand-picked from the rest of the bunch. This is a special job for the kids—the pick-up, that is, taking the cars, driving them off and dumping them somewhere. It pays ten dollars a trip, and it's a big honor besides. Billy-the-Mush never makes it. They always keep him out with a bucket, and he always has to carry the bucket while his partner makes the sale, or whatever they call it."

She reached toward the coffee pot to pour herself another cup, then took the brandy glass instead.

"The wash gang, you see," she went on, "have all the cars in a block spotted. Maybe they have a chalk code they mark on the tires or something. I don't know about that. But Duke knows which cars are unlocked, which ones have the key still in the ignition, and so on. Besides that, Woody has a full set of masters and a pocketful of jumpers for under the dash. Those kids can get into a locked car and drive it away in less than two minutes.

"Woody takes over here. Duke tells him how long a car has been parked, whatever they know concerning the likelihood of the owner returning, and so on. Woody picks the car that's to be taken, and drops the kid a block or so away, with instructions as to where it's to be driven. Later he picks the kid up near the place where the car has been abandoned. The wash crew is always in the clear—they are kept right in the neighborhood and told to make themselves conspicuous whenever a pick-up is being made in their sector. Maybe they get into an argument with a store-keeper, maybe they make a nuisance of themselves some other way. What they do doesn't matter, so long as it's apparent that they didn't drive the car away."

"Ten dollars a pick-up ..." Tom was frowning. "That represents ten wash jobs. It doesn't sound as though there could be much to be made that way."

"All I know is that Woody and Duke are both driving cars and that they don't appear to be lacking cash. Duke threw an even hundred dollars in my face last night. I mean—well, I guess I've been riding him pretty hard about not having a job and not helping out with expenses. He came in while I was getting dinner, went to his room for a while, and then put his head into the kitchen just long enough to toss a wad of bills on the table. And then he went out. You know Duke. The way he's been, I mean."

Tom whistled. "A hundred dollars!" Then he said. "Do you suppose these youngsters know that, technically, they're guilty of grand larceny whenever they drive off in a car valued at more than a thousand dollars?"

"I think Woody has them hypnotized into believing that so long as they just abandon the cars somewhere it doesn't matter. They think of it as being sort of a joke, as though every day were Hallowe'en. But what am I going to do, Tom? What am I going to do about Duke?"

"The question is bigger than that, Peg. Other teen-agers are involved. We've got to consider them. If it came to a showdown, whom would they follow—Duke or Woody?"

"I can't answer that. I don't know them that well. They accept Duke as leader, but they know that Woody is his boss. I suppose that if Woody and Duke disagreed, some would stick with Duke and some would be on Woody's side."

"Then I suggest that first of all you try to throw a scare into Duke. Talk to him, let him know you understand the whole set-up and what's going on. Hint that you have inside information that the police are getting ready to crack down on the racket. Maybe he'll pull out. Maybe he and Woody will talk it over and decide that it's getting too hot—which would be enough to break the thing up. For all we know, they may be ready to drop the whole business at the first sign of trouble."

"That's one thing they haven't had so far. Trouble, you know, Tom, not one of those kids has been picked up while taking a car. No one has ever noticed the cars being driven away, or at least they've never taken sufficient notice to be suspicious. They've all been clean jobs."

"This Woody must be a clever fellow in his line. I always wonder why a man like that can't try something useful instead. The chances are he'd make out even better in something legitimate."

"Look at Duke. He's intelligent, and he has the sort of imagination and talent that would probably make him a first-rate architect in time. Can you explain why he should do something like this?"

"No ... But it will all work out, Peggy," Tom reassured her. "Try spooking Duke off, first. If that doesn't do the trick, we'll go on from there. It isn't the end of the world, you know. He hasn't got into serious trouble yet, and the situation isn't anywhere near being out of hand. I'm reluctant to step in where Duke is concerned because he already thinks I'm a nosey old busybody, but if it becomes necessary, I will. And I promise you this—if he doesn't straighten out by himself, I'll straighten him out, whether he likes it or not. You've probably never seen an old bear with cubs, but I have, up in Canada. She'll let them raise hell, pull all sorts of pranks, but when they reach the point of endangering themselves she gives them a cuff that knocks them can over tea kettle. Well, that's how I am with kids, too."

Peggy suddenly giggled. "Haven't you got something mixed up? I can see you as the furry old patriarch, grumbling and growling, but not as the harassed hausfrau worrying over her children. Where's your apron?"

Tom grinned at her, obviously glad to see this change in her spirit.

"Patriarchal, am I? Well, I won't dispute it. Probably I ought to be on exhibition in the museum, along with the rest of the fossils."

"You know I didn't mean it like that. You're a long way from being old. In fact, I don't think you'll ever be old. I have a feeling about you that you never were young, either. I mean young like these kids."

"You ought to see my photo album, then. You'd be disillusioned if you saw me in a striped blazer, smoking a bulldog pipe. I went through all of it myself. My generation had its own catchwords, its own sharpies. I was a real-twenty-three-skiddoo kid."

"I never understood that twenty-three-skidoo business. Did it mean anything?"

"About as much as jive-talk does today. There used to be, and for all I know, still is, a terrific cross-wind at Twenty-third Street in New York, from the Hudson to the East River. The Flatiron Building seemed to funnel it somehow and make it stronger. Every day a bunch of idlers would gather in front of the building to watch the girls go by, with the wind lifting their skirts. And finally a cop would come along and tell them to skiddoo. An exposed calf was quite a shocking thing in those days."

The brandy glass was being refilled again. Peggy poured herself another cup of coffee, but it was cold now, and she put it aside with a wrinkle-nosed expression of distaste.

"It's hard to relate you to a time like that," she said. "It's like something out of one of those old newsreels they show on television."

Tom threw back his head and laughed.

"Really, Peg, I don't remember it either. I'm just repeating what I've been told. How old do you think I am? I didn't move in with the last glaciers, you know."

Peggy was feeling a bit giddy. Everything was beginning to take on a tinge of friendly humor, and she had lost that hard knot of nervous tension she had been carrying.

"I dig you the most, man," she said.

"What?"

"That's something Duke says. He and Woody are always digging something the most. Whatever it is, Duke digs it the most. And sometimes I think he doesn't really understand anything."

"Back there again? I thought we'd talked out the subject of Duke for this evening."

"We have. I'm not going to say another word about him, or even think of him. My nerves can't afford it. Tom, could we go outside? Walk in the garden, perhaps? I feel that I ought to have some air."

"Surely. Shall I turn on the floodlights? They don't give the same effect as sunlight, of course, but you can get some idea of what the flowers look like."

"I'd rather look at them some day when I can really see them. Now I just want to walk a bit."

When she stood up she found that she was somewhat unsteady on her feet. She felt within her an amusing lightness, pleasant even as it was surprising.

"Just a minute," she said. She turned up her glass, savoring the smooth sting of the liquor. "That's awfully good brandy."

CHAPTER THIRTEEN
CONSENT BY FORCE

THEY WENT OUT on the terrace and along a flagstone path in the general direction of a greenhouse. The night was warm and the air a soft breeze which touched lightly at her hair, questioningly caressed her flushed cheek. There was no moon, but to the north a multitude of stars glittered in a dead-black sky, diamonds spilled carelessly on velvet. Southward, the sky was lightened, the stars lost in the reddish glow of the main part of the city.

In silence, and apparently without aim, they strolled the grounds. Tom stopped once to light a cigar; in the brief flare of flame Peggy studied his strong, heavy-boned face. His features wore the habitual enigmatic half-smile of a man confident of his direction and his abilities. He caught her watching him, and the smile became complete, affectionate. Then the light snapped off, and his face was once again masked in the semidarkness.

Before that tour was completed, however, Peggy came to realize that they were not really walking at random. Their seeming aimlessness was controlled, was under Tom's quiet authority. Gradually she saw that she was being led, although so subtly that the decisions seemed to be hers. There were things which Tom wanted her to see, things in which he had an unspoken pride; there were glimpses of beauty, such as the silhouette of a twisted tree against the sky, which he wanted to offer her in such a way that she might think she had discovered it for herself.

Authority.

There was an instinctive resistance to the word. Yet one could do worse, much worse, than submit to the authority of a man like Tom.

"Wait."

He had stopped and had taken a step or two off the path. He touched an electric switch unobtrusively fastened to a young maple. A bank of base-lights at the border of a large planting of rose bushes sprang up, bathing the massed blossoms in a sudden, almost brutal radiance.

"Lovely," Peggy murmured.

"My gardener's idea. He has a completely free hand with the grounds. I don't even offer suggestions any more. After he'd been with me a month or so I suddenly realized that I had accidentally hired an artist—a true artist, who happened to work with growing things as his material. So I stay out of his way and meekly appreciate the beautiful things he creates for me."

Taking his penknife, he cut a rose and brought it to her. She drank its fragrance with her nostrils, nosing hungrily into the peppery scent, then capriciously wove the stem into her hair.

"I'm drunk, Tom," she said.

"I didn't know that. You don't act that way."

"But I know. I don't mean messy drunk. Happy drunk. Things are dislocated, that's all. New perspectives."

"That isn't drunk."

"All right. I have a glow on."

He snapped off the lights and took her arm. They walked to a huge oak, around the base of which a circular bench had been built. She stumbled once; Tom's strong grip was quick to aid her.

Leaning back against the rough bark of the tree, she took a deep breath which escaped as a relaxed sigh. The stars above were lovely and friendly, but it was hard to separate them individually. They appeared in pairs; groups became streaks if she looked at them for more than a few seconds. The phenomenon was more interesting than annoying, and she quickly became lost in her study of it.

"Peggy."

Tom's voice was at once far away and very near. His hand sought hers, the warm strength of his fingers firm against her softly yielding palm.

"Yes, dear."

She was mildly surprised at herself. The word had slipped out with no warning, quite thoughtlessly.

"There's something I must say, and yet I'm almost afraid to say it. I've had a glimpse of something which could be very wonderful, and I want it. But I'm frightened of spoiling, of changing, what I have now."

"I can't imagine you being frightened of anything."

"But I am. I've never been afraid to approach a gamble before—possibly because I never stood to lose anything which couldn't be replaced. Once I've said this, though, everything between us will be changed. If you reject what I ask, I may find that I have lost something I cannot afford to lose—the relationship which exists here and tonight. I love you, Peggy."

"Yes."

"I love you, and I want you to be my wife."

"Tom."

"I need you to stay here and be with me." The words were a rush, now. "I am asking you to marry me. I will try very, very hard to make you happy. I cannot promise anything further than that, but I will try."

He leaned toward her, his caress tentative, hesitant. And that hesitation surprised her more than the fact that he was proposing marriage. Whatever Tom wanted was usually gone after boldly, aggressively.

"I don't know, Tom … I can't say yes. Not now. And I don't want to say no."

"You don't love me, is that it?"

"I didn't say that. It's just that I can't be sure I could ever be any man's wife. You saw what happened to me the other night. I wasn't having a sudden seizure of conscience. I just couldn't go on with it"

"I see. I thought I'd frightened you in some way."

"No. I frighten myself. I have to be honest with you, Tom— that wasn't the first time. In Paris there was a young man I thought I loved, and perhaps did. It was the same with him. In fact I was trying very hard to give up my virginity when I received your call from America."

"Darling …"

All hesitation gone, he swept her into his arms and kissed her mouth, long and hard. Then, while she clung desperately to him, he tried to reassure her. It was a common enough problem, he told her. One with which any qualified therapist could surely cope.

"I may have to enter analysis to get rid of it," she admitted. "But first I'd like to try once more. Maybe I'd only succeed in driving my spooks somewhere else, but if I only managed to do that, I could at least function as—as some man's wife."

"You mean you want to …"

"Will you help me to try, Tom? Please? Look, I'm not completely frigid, dead to passion. At this moment I want you. I really, truly do. And that wanting will go on building up, go on and on until I think I can't stand it for another instant—and then I hit that stone wall and get panicked. Being held by you this way, touched by you, and kissed—I'm in a fever, can't you tell? My thighs—they're burning. And this is just the beginning. Soon I'll be feeling like—like a cat in heat. Here, give me your hand … there! Does that happen if a woman is cold to love?"

She squirmed sensuously in his arms like a small, excited animal. Her voice thickened with instinctive hungers, lowered to an intimate, suggestive whisper.

"Please help me, Tom. Take me. I want to be had … by you …"

He stood up, bringing her to her feet with him. With his arm about her waist he led her back to the house.

Back in that huge living room, her eye immediately went to the decanter. Noticing, Tom poured another drink.

"It relaxes me," she explained. "And that seems to be the whole secret—I've got to relax completely. I'm sorry that it's also making me drunk. That doesn't seem very flattering to you. But then, drunken women are supposed to be more exciting, aren't they? More wanton, with their inhibitions off guard?"

"Don't worry about that. Are you sure, though, that this is what you want?"

"Does it make you think less of me? Is the foolish virgin throwing in her chance of an advantageous marriage?"

"Do you take me for a simple jackass? Or a complicated one?"

"Then, yes, it's what I want. It's more than that. It's what I've got to have. I'm putting myself in your hands."

"You mean that last?"

"Completely. Because I've got to, you see. I can't trust myself. If I hesitate, if I become resistant—well, somebody's got to be in the driver's seat. I'll try to do whatever you say, but if I refuse …"

She did not finish. A glance at his face told her that he understood her meaning. She was depending on him to lead her, to furnish authority if it were needed. Had ever a girl, she wondered, told her lover such a thing before? Perverts, perhaps. Women who confused sex with punishment, whose pleasure was dependent upon pain and beatings, whose desire required the simulation of rape. But she was not one of those. She had no desire to be hurt or brutally treated. This was more in the nature of a tooth extraction before the days of anesthetics. One asked to be strapped down and rendered helpless against whatever needed to be done, seeking final relief, but certainly not enjoyment of the pain. And yet, tenuous as a wisp of smoke was a curious, curling pleasure in the thought of submission ...

Tom had turned out most of the lights in the room. There was a soft glow from a part of the indirect ceiling lights, and one bulb of a lamp near the radio was still burning. The effect was nearly that of the candlelight over which they had finished dinner. The music now was a sequence of Beethoven quartettes.

Tom seated himself in a large, wing-back chair, and with his penknife snipped off the end of a cigar which he obviously had no thought of finishing. Was that heavily masculine gesture a consciously contrived bit of staging, she wondered, intended to underline the role he had been asked to play?

"Take off your clothes," he said quietly.

Like that. Casually, almost. But not quite casually. He meant it. He expected it to be done.

"But—here? Right here in the living room? What about the servants?"

He did not answer her. He leaned back in the chair and put the cigar to his mouth and waited.

She looked toward the room's windows.

"What if a car should drive up? What if someone came?"

He still said nothing, but sat watching her. On his face, if there was expression at all, there was a faint question.

The windows again. Already, without having made a move, she felt naked, watched by a dozen pairs of alien, sniggering eyes. She was being forced into an indignity before an unknown audience, and she was resentful. It was unfair of Tom to do this to her, to expect her to strip herself in a lighted living room, exposing her body and her passion to any casual passerby. Did he *want* her to be seen? Was that, perhaps, some sort of punishment for having told him honestly of her need? She wouldn't do it! She—

"Take off your clothes."

He had not raised his voice. He had used the tone, rather, of one who has given an order not immediately understood.

She wouldn't! She—

"Yes, Tom."

There was the soft rip of a zipper, the rustle of light cloth. With the excessive precision of drunkenness, she folded her dress over her arm—and then dropped it to the floor. Suddenly she had that sense of what the French call *déjà vu*—she had been there before. So had she stood in a little apartment in Paris, so had she looked up at the man who was watching her then. There the man had been younger, less an authority figure—weaker, perhaps. And the panties had been canary yellow rather than aqua; the garter-belt straps had been appliqued with roses. The shoes, it happened, were the same. She had been there before, and had known this same sense of excited dread.

She felt for the snaps of her brassiere. No way of folding *that*. She let it fall with the dress and turned back to Tom, her strong young breasts lifting in protesting pride against the shame of their nakedness.

"Do you want me to go out on the street to finish this?" she asked. "Is that what you want? Because, I'll tell you now—I'll do it! Perhaps you thought I was making some sort of a bluff, and you wanted to call my hand. But when I told you how it had to be,

I meant it! I'll try to do whatever you say, and if I freeze up, you can depend on it—I won't be pulling an act!"

A short time before there had been only tenderness and warmth between them; now she faced him almost as an adversary in some combat. She knew that neither her actions nor her words were quite logical. She was saying both too much and too little, and what she wanted to convey was not being expressed. But *why* had he done this to her?

Tom put aside his cigar and smiled at her.

"Come here."

She went to him and he drew her down upon his lap. She sat stiffly on his knees, the bare undersides of her thighs twitching at the rough, almost hairy feel of his trousers.

"All right," he admitted. "It was a sort of test—to see if you'd go along with me despite what your own feelings said. You needn't worry about the servants. I insist upon my own privacy and respect theirs. They come and go by a door at the far wing of the house, and their quarters are well removed from mine. As for being surprised or spied upon, that's impossible. The drive gate is closed now, and an alarm system would sound if someone attempted to enter the grounds."

She allowed her head to be drawn down upon his deep chest. His hands and lips began to intimately question her body. The tenseness began to seep away. And some time after that, curling one finger in a lock of his startlingly gray hair, she whispered:

"Promise you'll *make* me, Tom," she whispered. "No matter what I say, or how I act, or what I do. But, please kiss me too, if you can. I may fight. I don't know what may happen. I know that I want you now, and I'm putting myself wholly in your hands."

She turned in his arms, her hips gleaming whitely.

Later there was a couch in a corner, and darkness save for the greenish luminescence of the radio dial-face. Whisperings and silences, and the thrusting sound of insistent movement. Once a whimpering, a choked-off protest, and the sudden, startling strike of an angry palm on soft flesh. And through the whimpering, the words:

"Make me! Oh, darling, dearest! *Make* me!"

Finally she shared his bedroom for the rest of the night. It was only the first of several such nights.

CHAPTER FOURTEEN
YOUNG COUPLE

T OM WANTED THEM to be married immediately. He brought
the subject up next morning, while the butler, as implacably
impersonal as when he had left them, served breakfast.

"It's too soon, Tom," Peggy objected. "Too soon for a lot of
reasons. First of all, people would talk if I married so shortly
after my father's death. I don't care for myself—Mike would have
laughed at such an idea—but it wouldn't be good for you. Your
political enemies would snatch at any sort of gossip to hurt you."

"Let them try," he smiled, as he squeezed a few drops of
lemon into his tomato juice. "Do you like Worcestershire with
this stuff?"

"No. But I'm right, and you know I am. And besides that, I
feel that we ought to be more or less engaged for a while. After all,
how well do we really know each other?"

He cocked a sardonic eyebrow at her, and she blushed furi-
ously, bowing her head over coffee which was still too hot.

"You know what I mean," she said in a very small voice. A
timid voice, almost. "What happened last night was a wonderful
thing for me. It made me feel that I'm really a woman, at last.
But—suppose you find that I bore you? What if I don't like the
same books, the same pictures, the same music as you? In that
sense, I think we ought to know each other better. A lifetime is a

long time, Tom. No, let's not set a date yet. We've no reason to be in a rush, have we?"

"Just as you want it, Peg," he said.

"I—" She broke off as the butler returned with a tray of tiny sausages, bacon, eggs and toast. When the man had left she said to Tom, "He embarrasses me. I don't seem to be able to assume the right attitude toward servants. They remain people to me. He opened the door when I came in yesterday evening; he'll close it when I leave. And he knows that only one bed was slept in last night."

"You needn't worry about Carter's discretion. He doesn't point the finger at anyone. You see—well, Carter isn't a regular butler, if there is any such thing as a regular butler. I've never told anyone this before, but I can't very well keep anything from you, can I? Carter is an ex-con. Five years for forgery, and couldn't get a job when he got out. I took him on, and he seems to like it this way. At least, on the few occasions when I've run into something else that he might do, he's always turned it down."

Peggy stared out the window toward the reservoir, symbolic of Tom's job, reflecting now a thick golden glow in the morning sun.

"You're a strange man, Tom," she said. "Your life is lived on so many levels. Yesterday you were advising a high-ranking army official on matters which I'm sure were confidential, yet you trust an ex-convict with the freedom of your home. A chauffeur drives you about in a limousine, but you know how a case of mumps is progressing in the family of a shoemaker on the other side of the tracks."

"The important thing," he pointed out, "is that the shoemaker doesn't resent the limousine. On the contrary, it gives him a sense of confidence. He feels more secure. If he needs help, he knows where to turn. The man in the limousine has all sorts of omnipotent and mysterious powers. The cobbler's faith would certainly be greatly shaken if I shuffled about the streets in frayed trousers and broken shoes. Call this paternalism; is it necessarily bad?"

"I don't know. There's something confusing in the idea."

"Consider it this way, then—do you resent anything that happened last night?"

"No." She gave this some thought. "Perhaps I did at the moment. Not now."

"Yet there were times when your actions were not those of your own free will or choosing."

"That's putting it mildly." She felt her cheeks flushing again, and became quickly attentive to her plate. For she had been punished like a child when she did not obey his demands. She had been subjected to indignity upon indignity—for indignities they had been to her outraged, resistant senses at the time.

"Yet you gave up your freedom of choice in advance. In fact, you were highly insistent upon that point."

"Yes."

"And you don't regret having done that?"

"No!" A vaguely remembered phrase from something she had once read in her college days, when she had had time to read, came to mind. It was probably D. H. Lawrence; if it wasn't, it should have been. Something about thinking that one would die of shame, but the shame died instead. Except in her case the shame was not completely dead. At the same time, even in that shame, she had become radiant, known ecstasy, been filled and completed and finally, rapturously exhausted.

"No," she repeated, "I gained a whole new world."

She looked across the table at the characteristically half-smiling face of the man who had last night been—yes, her master. And then she was thinking of Jacques. If the phone had not interrupted, if they had been together for another hour … But Jacques had been more a boy than a man. He could never have been firm in the way that Tom was, could never have bent her to an inflexible male will while she cried out in protest. He had been too soft, too sensitive. Somewhere about the flat, she remembered, there was an unanswered letter. She must find it and read it. She had been so terribly busy …

Tom's smile did not disappear even when he frowned, when his face showed annoyance because he could not immediately find the foot buzzer with which to summon the butler for something he wanted. The sun, striking obliquely through the panes, emphasized the massive dignity of his head, threw tones of gold into the bone-white of his hair.

This, then, was the man to whom she had completely given herself, to whom she was sure that she would entrust her whole future. She looked at him with a certain uneasy wonder at herself.

Authority.

John Fanson swung his nondescript sedan to the curb, shut off the engine, and leaned back to enjoy the last few drags of his cigaret.

"Well, here we go again," he said. "*Aria da capo.* Free translation: a cop's life sure is hell. How many blocks does this make so far?"

"I've lost count," Peggy said. "I didn't realize how many rooming houses there were in the city until now."

"You ain't seen the half of it, sister."

"Funny," she said, more to herself than to him.

"What?"

"Nothing important. I'm continually being surprised by people, that's all. They don't turn out to be what I expect them to be."

"I don't think it's cricket, old gel."

"All right, now it's my turn. What?"

"To throw off enigmatic remarks and leave a guy hanging. Especially a nice guy like I'm. What did you have in mind?"

"You, particularly. Half the time you talk like some South End character whose idea of elegance is suede shoes. And then you'll suddenly make some remark which makes it evident that you have a quite different set of values, and a wholly different way of thinking."

"Aw, somebody gave me a subscription to the *Reader's Digest* by mistake one Christmas. I got all cultured. And one day I went to the library to look up some old copies of the *Daily Racing Form,* only somebody got the wrong slip, and before I knew what was happening I had read three feet seven inches of Dr. Eliot's *Five-Foot Shelf.*"

"I wasn't being patronizing. I was wondering why."

"You wonder why a cop can't go around making like he's Oscar Wilde? You think I'd do better to turn in my badge for a nosegay?"

"I don't see why being a cop makes it necessary for you to pretend you're Mortimer Snerd. I don't like people who wear their precious culture like a boutonniere either, yet I can't see that one ought to be ashamed of having once read a book."

"Okay, let's talk culchered, like. First of all, I'll begin by admitting that I've got a B.A. degree kicking around in a trunk somewhere. It doesn't say any place that they'll ask for it back if they catch me saying 'ain't.' Secondly, I've written a volume of poetry which no one will publish, although the little mags have used some of it. I buy a painting once in a while, when my bank account will allow it, and I have a shameful secret vice—I enjoy ballet. I have a suspicion that what I really like is to look at the girls' legs under those frilly skirts, because I had a pretty good time when I went to burlesque, too. Not a completely good time, but a pretty good time."

"I've never seen a burlesque show."

"You ought to, some day. You won't enjoy some of it, but it's damned educational to study the audience. When they're working on a teaser for a full strip, you have a feeling that they'd like it better if a tiger came out and ate her. As for the ballet, there's a new group performance tonight that I want to see. Like to come with me?"

"Why ..." She was startled by the suggestion of a date coming from John Fanson. Their relationship so far had been only that of two people who happened to work together, and she had not believed that he had any interest in her further than that. And there was Tom, to whom she was practically engaged.

But not formally engaged. Not completely. And he was out of town for a couple of days. Besides which, there was no reason why she should not have other friends, male or female.

"Why ... yes," she finished.

"Good. But let's talk about it later. Right now we'd better get busy looking for those kids again."

They left the car and started down the mean street, resuming the canvass of cheap rooming houses on which they had been engaged for two days. Their questioning, through constant repetition, had become as formalized as the approach of a door-to-door salesman. An hour later they finally found what they had been looking for.

John Fanson tipped his hat to the thin-lipped, suspicious woman who answered the bell marked "Landlady."

"Routine police check-up, ma'am," he said, as she carefully studied his badge. "We're looking for a couple of youngsters who may have moved into this neighborhood in the last day or two. Maybe you can help us out."

"How do you mean, a couple of youngsters?"

"A girl and a young fellow. They're both under age. Although," he added quickly as he saw a guarded look come over her face, "they may look old enough to fool anybody. At any rate, some of the people along the street believe they've seen a couple answering their description, and they think they've been coming and going from this house. What can you tell us about it?"

"Who said that, about them being at this house? It was that stuck-up Mrs. Kerr next door, wasn't it? Wasn't it, now? Always tryin' to get somebody else in trouble, she is. Why, if I told you some of the things that go on in *her* place—"

"Then they are here?"

"I didn't say they was and I didn't say they wasn't. Always tryin' to get somebody in trouble, and her renting out to all sorts of tramps and floozies that come along. Men comin' and a-goin' at all hours, parties goin' on half the night, radios playin'—"

"Can we have a look at your record book, please?"

"My record book is in perfectly good order, young man. The police say I've got to keep a record of who moves in and out, I keep a record. I run a clean house, with no monkey business, and nobody can say any different. Not like some people I could mention, if I was the kind who wanted to talk about my neighbors."

"Are they in now?"

"What makes you so sure they live here, the ones you want? What do you want them for, anyway?"

"Well, they *do* live here, don't they? I think we'd better see that book, ma'am."

She moved reluctantly aside and led them down a gloomy hall.

"I did have a young couple move in day before yesterday," she said. "I never said I didn't. But they didn't look no different from any other young couple to me. I can't ask everybody who wants a room to show me their birth certificates, like they was getting screened by the F.B.I. or something. They signed the register, regular, and that's the best I can do. I'm not here to guess people's ages and weights, like it was an amusement part. I can't be responsible for anything they do outside of my house, either. What did they do, anyway?"

" 'Mr. and Mrs. Raymond Ross,' " John read. "Hell, the kid even used his right name."

"See! Everything regulation, just like I told you! That's the only way to run—"

"Yes, ma'am. What room do they have?"

"Two-E. Second floor, all the way back. You want I should come with you?"

"No, we'll see if they're in, first."

"Look, now, I done everything regular. The register book and everything. You saw that. This isn't going to make trouble for me, is it? Because I can't know what people are, or what they done. So long as they look all right to me, what more can I do?"

"I wouldn't say you were in trouble, ma'am. You might have to appear in court as a witness; I wouldn't know about that. But after this, maybe it would be a good idea for you to put on your glasses when you look over prospective tenants. That girl isn't sixteen yet."

They went up the dreary stairs, leaving the woman gasping with indignant protest.

"If they call through the door, you answer. They'll be more likely to open to a woman." Peggy nodded, and John added, "You'll find that most doors open a lot quicker if you rap out something that sounds like code. For some reason people, whatever their ages, assume that someone who raps out the old shave-and-a-hair-cut is a friend."

He flicked his knuckles across the door panel in such a way that the sound was a confused rhythm, neither heavy nor light. There was the rustle of quick, light footsteps, and then the door was thrown open.

The girl was slight, pretty, and radiant in her smile. She was blonde and glowing pink, and had evidently just stepped from her bath. And her blondeness was unquestionably natural. She was completely naked.

"Oh!" she exclaimed. The smile faded, and she tried to shut the door. John Fanson's foot jammed it. She slipped behind the door, trying to conceal herself as she shoved against it.

"Wrong apartment," she said in a high, frightened voice. "You have the wrong apartment."

"Just a minute, miss," John Fanson said. "We want to talk to you."

"You don't want to talk to me. You have the wrong apartment."

"I don't think so. Are you Mrs. Raymond Ross?"

"I—I—why?" She thrust her blonde head and one shoulder around the edge of the door. Unknown to her, one young, budding breast, the nipple as pink and tender as a spring strawberry, was also revealed for a brief instant.

"The landlady says you're Mrs. Ross. We want to talk to you."

"I don't ... I ... Just a minute."

She evidently did not realize that the pier glass on a closet door reflected her image as, with the awkward grace of adolescence, she crossed the room and put on a man's bathrobe which was lying across a chair. Despite the seriousness of the situation, Peggy had to smile as she glanced sideways at her partner. He was self-consciously fingering the knot of his tie.

The girl came back to the door, fastening the belt around her waist.

"What was it you wanted?" she asked. The question was directed to Peggy, and it was unsure, affected and young-sounding.

"May we come in? We'd like to speak to you privately," Peggy said. And then, "We're police, Christine."

"Police! You ... Do you have a warrant?" Her blue eyes were wide in panic.

"So you know that much, already," John said. "And, as usual, know it wrong. We're not here to search the premises. There's an on-sight pick-up order out for you and Raymond, Christine."

He followed Peggy into the room, then pushed the door back, leaving it slightly ajar.

"Where's Raymond, Christine?"

She was scared, and it showed. She sat down on the wobbly bed and looked at them.

"I don't know what this is all about. I'm not going to say anything. You don't have any right ... any right to ... to ..."

"You don't have to say anything," John told her. "That's your privilege. All we want is an identification. Are you Christine Liscomb?"

"I—no. I'm Mrs.—I won't say. You have no right."

"Somebody has the right, Christine. You're not old enough to be Mrs. anybody—not under the laws of this state, nor of the state you came from."

Even in her fright, a brief glint of amusement lighted the girl's eyes.

"I'm not?" she asked. "You mean that one of these days—at twelve midnight plus one second—I'll be smarter, or something? Then I'll be ready to be Mrs. Somebody-or-other? What do you want from me, you people?"

"Where's Raymond?"

"I don't know. He's not here. Why don't you look for him?" She noticed John looking at her pale thighs, and she drew the bathrobe about her knees. Then she said to Peggy, "Are you Mrs. Somebody? Is there something I've done wrong in trying to be a wife?"

"We're not here to discuss who or what is right or wrong," John said. "That's not our business. Just get dressed, please. They want to talk to you downtown."

"What if I won't? Suppose I say that anybody who wants to talk to me has to come here, instead of me going to them?"

"That wouldn't be very smart, Christine. It wouldn't do you a bit of good. It could do you a lot of harm. You've got to realize that you're under arrest now."

"What for? What have I done? I haven't done anything to hurt anybody. Why don't you—"

"Go out and catch some criminals," Peggy finished for her. "Look, Christine, we have orders to arrest you, and all the argument in the world can't change that. Now, are you going to tell us where we can find Raymond?"

"I don't know where he is. You'll have to look for him, I guess."

"We won't have to look far—or long," John said dryly. "I'm pretty sure you're expecting him any minute. It doesn't strike me that you're the sort of girl who answers the door naked to anyone who knocks."

CHAPTER FIFTEEN
THE WAYWARD ONES

THE WORDS were scarcely out of his mouth when the door swung inward.

"Hey, baby, I—"

The boy broke off in mid-sentence, looking at the three of them without expression. He was a good-looking boy, Peggy noted, with a firm, self-reliant lift of chin, a tight pride in his carriage. It was not difficult to imagine him on the high school football gridiron or swimming the 100-meter free-style. In fact, she suddenly realized, it was not difficult to imagine him as a bed partner. There was a strong aura of healthy, lusty sexuality about his personality. He was as vital as a young bull, and that vitality was apparent in every line of his rather short, thick-muscled body.

John Fanson was not impressed.

"Hello, Raymond," he said. "We were expecting you."

"They're from the police, Ray," the girl said quickly.

The boy nudged the door shut with his elbow, and crossed the room with the bag of groceries he was carrying. He set the bag on a small table next to the two-burner gas plate, and lifted a box of eggs out.

"It didn't take you long," he said. "Are we under arrest?"

"Yes."

"How did you get on us so fast? Or is that a professional secret?"

"It's not a secret," John said. "Runaway kids usually head for the nearest big city. The rest was just a matter of checking up."

The boy went over to the bed on which Christine was sitting, ran his hand affectionately through her hair.

"Ray," she said. "Ray, I'm scared. What will they do?"

"Don't worry, baby," he said.

She grasped his hand, took it to her lips and kissed his fingers.

"Will they send me home, Ray? Can they make me go back there?"

"Baby, this is just part of it. We'll make it somehow. No matter what. We'll make it."

"Raymond," John Fanson said, "you just asked me a question and I answered it. Now, will you answer one for me? You look like a couple of nice kids. Why the hell did you have to get yourselves in a jam? Why couldn't you have waited until you could get married, and do the thing properly? I'm not asking that as a cop, now, and you don't have to answer. I'm just wondering."

Raymond, standing beside the girl, looked at the detective as though he were mentally measuring him, weighing his chances of a direct, physical attack. Then he shrugged.

"You called us runaway kids," he said. "Does it say anywhere in whatever papers you have on us, what we were running away from?"

"A pick-up order doesn't include a life history, Raymond. We know that you were both in high school, and we know that you used to work part time in a garage in your town."

"I'm a good mechanic," Raymond said. "In fact—why should I run myself down?—I'm a *damned* good mechanic. I figured that I could get a job here and we'd be all set."

"What were you running away from?" Peggy asked. "Why couldn't you wait?"

The boy's eyes were hard as flint as he looked at her.

"You couldn't leave us alone, though, could you?" he said. "We couldn't have a chance to make it, and live like decent people, the way we wanted to."

"Ray," the girl said. "Ray, don't make them mad. I'm afraid."

"I know you're afraid. You're always afraid, and that's part of it."

"They won't understand. It doesn't matter."

"The hell it doesn't! What have we done, that we should have to creep around and crawl? You're not going to crawl, baby—not while you're with me. You're going to stand up and yell back at things."

He took her wrist and drew her to her feet.

"Show them," he said.

"Please, Ray ..."

"Show them, damn it! If you won't, I will!" He turned to John, anger burning brightly in his eyes. "You don't have to look at this, mister. I'm not showing her off for sale. But I want the lady to know what I'm talking about."

He ripped the bathrobe roughly down over the girl's shoulders, disregarding her cry of protest, and threw it into a corner. Completely nude, the girl bowed her head as, with one arm about her shoulder, he turned her so as to expose her back. Peggy gasped, for now she saw something which, in her earlier surprise at the girl's nakedness she had not noticed. From shoulder to calves, Christine's body was welted, viciously streaked with markings which ranged in color from a flaming red to a greenish blue. There were dark bruises on the backs of her thighs, thick stains of discoloration about the young, taut swell of her hips.

"Turn around."

The girl tried to cover her face with her hands, but the boy pulled her arms down to her side.

"No," he said. "Look at them. And see if they can look back at you. They're cops, and came to arrest us because we're breaking the law."

"Just a minute—" John began.

"To hell with you. I said you didn't have to look. You getting a kick out of this? You enjoying it?"

The girl's small breasts were lined and striped with the marks of a vindictive, slashing beating. Her white belly was laced with that pattern of hatred, and the criss-cross markings moved snake-like down the fronts of her thighs to her knees.

"That's what we're running away from," Raymond said. "Every Saturday night he puts a strap to her, her stepfather. For no reason at all. Only he lays it on heavier when he's been drunk and tried to get her into bed. Not just alone. With her mother— that's the way he'd like it, with both of them together. He's beaten her mother down to where she'd do anything. And that's what we're running away from, copper."

"Please, Ray." Christine was crying now. "What are you doing to me?"

"I'm trying to get these people to understand what it's all about, that's all."

"Can I get dressed now, Ray?"

"Put on your blue dress. I like that one."

She tried to smile. "I guess it's as good a dress as any to be arrested in."

"Raymond," John Fanson said, "I think you and I could just as well wait out in the hall."

"Yeah, okay." The boy looked at the detective for a moment, and then he said, "Thanks."

They left the room. In the hallway John slouched against the wall while the boy paced nervously up and down.

"You carry a gun, Raymond?"

"No."

"Sure?"

"Sure I'm sure! I took out a hunting license last year, and I went out for rabbits twice, with a borrowed shotgun. Anything else?"

"I'm trying to help you, fellow. I don't like this any more than you do."

"I don't own a gun. I don't carry one. You want to search me?"

"I don't think so."

"Listen," the boy said. "I don't care about myself. I can take it, whatever it is. But you saw how she is, the way she's scared. What will they do to her?"

"I don't know, Raymond. I'm a cop, not the court."

"But you must have some idea! Look—if they lock her up, she'll go to pieces, you can see that, can't you?"

"I'm sorry, fellow. I guess you should have looked ahead a little further before you took off."

"There wasn't any chance to look in any direction. She had to get out of that."

"You tell the court what you told us, Raymond. If what you said is the truth, any judge will give it a great deal of consideration."

"Consideration—that's great. And what do you mean, *if* it's true? You don't think I did that to her, do you?"

"No, I don't think you did. Whoever is responsible for that stands to have a hell of a lot of explaining to do."

"You mean they'll go after the old man?"

"Probably."

"But damn it, he's the one who set the cops on us! He must be."

"Then that was his mistake. What about your own folks?"

"All I got is an uncle. He doesn't bother much about what I do, and I left him a note, I said I'd write. But look, now everybody back home is going to know, aren't they? I mean what went on around there, and what was happening to her. That's nice for her, isn't it?"

"The court will appoint someone to look after her interests and decide how best to handle things."

The door opened and Peggy said, "I guess we're ready."

"What about our things?" the boy asked.

"They'll be taken care of."

"I'll bet. I can imagine how that landlady will take care of them."

They found that good person waiting on the landing below.

"Tramps!" she exclaimed. "Nasty little tramps, making trouble for my house! If I'd known—"

"That's enough," John said. "Now, listen to what I've got to say. Two-E is locked. It's to stay that way. It is not to be entered for any reason by you or anyone else, except by police authority or the permission of Raymond Ross. The rent, I understand, is paid for two weeks. Someone will be around before that."

"You mean, looking for clues, like? What did they do, anyway?"

John Fanson laid his finger along his nose and looked mysterious.

"Guard those clues," he said, "with your very life."

The anonymous, rather dispirited-looking sedan rolled slowly toward the red traffic light, then darted ahead at the flash of green.

"One thing about that kid," John chuckled, "he wasn't bulling when he said he knows motors. He knew right away that I've got a souped-up job under the hood. He even figured out what had been done to bring it up."

"What's going to happen to them, John?"

"Reformatory, I guess. What the hell else can they do with youngsters like that. They can't send the girl back to the kind of a deal she was getting, so she'll have to put in some time at a Home for Wayward Girls, as they're called in her state. His will be an Industrial School for Boys. It won't be too rough. They're minors, so they won't get the book."

"Rough enough."

"Yeah. Technically, though, look what they could be hit with. They crossed a state line for purposes which, lacking a better term, we must call immoral, so you have a violation of the Mann Act right there. She's under age, so you add contributing to the delinquency of a minor and statutory rape to his charge. Tie in half a dozen laws, in two states, which have to do with fornication and adultery and unlawful cohabitation. In the state they come from, they have a charge called lascivious carriage, and it doesn't have anything with how you swing your hips when you walk, either. It covers everything from fellation to solitary vice, public consort, prostitution, and mopery, so I guess it covers the night they spent at a hotel before they crossed the line."

"What's mopery?"

"Nothing. A joke. It's supposed to be the act of exposing one's self to a blind woman on a public highway."

"Some joke. Now, what will they really do to that girl?"

"Probably charge her with being in manifest danger of falling into habits of vice."

"What's that again?"

"It doesn't say anything at all, but that's the way they have it on the books. They don't have to prove that she did anything except—well, be in manifest danger, and so forth and so forth. It's supposed to be for her own protection. They pull her out of a bad situation before she's gotten into trouble, or been forced into trouble. A situation such as her home life."

"The boy had already pulled her out of that, hadn't he? What they were trying to do—was that vice? Was that vicious? It looked to me as though they were pretty good to each other, and for each other."

"I don't make the laws, Malone, and neither do you—at least, not directly. There's some pretty wild stuff on the books. Ordinances against shooting pigeons from street cars, blue laws that prescribe exactly how, when, and in what position a man may make love to his wife. But in a case like this, nine times out of ten the book is right. Maybe they would have managed to get along, but the odds were against them. What would they have done when their money ran out, if they couldn't get jobs? Suppose she became pregnant, and they had to worry about that? A couple of kids, with no one to turn to, can became pretty desperate in that kind of a situation. Maybe we've saved them from something a hell of a lot worse than what they're up against now. I hope so, anyway. I have to hope so, or I couldn't stay on this job."

CHAPTER SIXTEEN
GUILTY FEELINGS

THIS WAS THE NIGHT of Peggy's date with John to see the ballet. The time passed pleasantly, though without any special incident, until they were leaving the theatre.

"I'm drunk," Peggy said. "Drunk with motion." She sighed deeply as John took the glowing lighter from the dashboard and touched it to her cigarette. "Ever since we left the theatre I've been pitying the people plodding along the streets, wondering why they didn't dance. It would be such a wonderful world if everyone danced! But instead—well, right now I really understand the meaning of the word 'pedestrian.'"

"I know," John said. "There's a feeling that you've had a glimpse into a different life, a world with new dimensions. That's why the theatre is fun."

"Will you come up for a drink? I have only some port—but it's good port. And there's some chicken asking to be made into sandwiches."

"I love chicken."

"Then why are we waiting?" She got out of the car and spun in a pirouette across the sidewalk. Glancing up, she saw that the windows of the flat were dark. Duke wasn't in. He seldom was, now.

She took John upstairs and left him sitting on the sofa while she went to the kitchen and found an apron. She made sandwiches and took them into the small living room, putting the tray down on a coffee table she had made from a large piece of flagstone. As she poured the wine she found herself thinking of Tom's home, comparing that expansive, impeccably appointed room in which she had first, and half a dozen times since, wantonly given herself, with the meager, cramped comfort of this place in which she had lived most of the years she could remember.

"It ought to be white," she apologized for the wine. "Or Burgundy, at least. But I haven't been thinking about things like that recently."

"So we'll bypass regulation," John said. "Maybe I don't know nothin' about art, but I know what I like. I like this."

Later—perhaps half an hour later—his arm was about her shoulder as they sat together on the sofa. And then he was kissing her. She had known that would happen. But she didn't quite know what to do about it. So, for the time being, she did nothing.

He kissed her, and she liked it. She liked the strong pull of his arms drawing her toward him, the hot, seeking bite of his mouth on her moist lips. She liked the insistent press of his body to hers, the squeezing, smothering crush when her breasts were thrown against his hard chest. She liked it, but she felt guilty.

It wasn't fair to Tom. The moment his back was turned, she was in another man's arms. And this astonished her. What sort of a woman was she? She thought briefly of little Christine Liscomb, who wanted so much to be a wife, and she was ashamed.

But it had happened so easily, so naturally, so—rightly. One moment they had been talking together, laughing over some anecdote, and an instant later she was passively accepting his embrace, the strong demand of his kiss. Passively? Not quite. Just at first, perhaps. Then she was participating, kissing him back.

One could find explanations, or invent them. In the weeks that she had known John Fanson, she had learned to admire him. Learned to admire him in the way that she had admired Mike. Wasn't it also possible that, in that time, she had fallen somewhat in love, without knowing it—or at least have become, unconsciously, sexually attracted? And then there was the factor of the evening's excitement, which she had already termed a kind of intoxication. The taut, young bodies of the male dancers, their masculinity so evident beneath the skin-tight costuming, had undoubtedly contributed a strong stimulation.

And what did this all add up to? Until she had met Jacques, no man had truly excited her. Since then it seemed that any man who wanted to could kiss her, and that any man who kissed her could raise her passion to fever pitch. Was she then to be any man's woman, so long as he was forceful enough, and insistent enough, to take her? Was that her role—to be used by anyone who was strong enough to disregard protest? She knew the phrases: "round heels" ... "a push-over." *Was* she a push-over, if the man only pushed hard enough? And what significance, if any, was there in the fact that sexuality had awakened in her only after Mike had been laid in his grave?

She wasn't ready to really consider that last question. To the others, she had to answer yes. If she were incapable of fidelity, of remaining steadfastly faithful to one man, now was the time to face it, before her affair with Tom went any further. Tom deserved—anyone deserved—a better deal than to find himself married to someone who couldn't help catting around, someone who was a juicy red apple for whoever knew how to shake the tree.

"John, we shouldn't. John ... John, no ..."

But John Fanson, in his own way, was also a man who knew what he wanted, and who did not hesitate to go after it. In those next few moments, while her resistance to his more and more intimate knowledge of her body ebbed away, she began to under-stand the firm determination which underlay the tolerant mild-ness of his manner. As though it were a game in which two others were involved, she watched the contest of her conscience matched against his will. It was symbolized, perhaps, by the upward prog-ress of her skirt as it was drawn about her knees, along her thighs. The stockings she wore were very sheer and of extra length; their tops came far up her legs. Yet the picture she had of herself as he leaned across her to pull the lamp chain included several inches of those white, waiting thighs.

Then there was darkness, and her quick, urgent gasp ...

The rattle of a key at the door brought her back to reality. She sat up, tugging at her panties, pulled down her skirt and turned on the light. Duke came into the flat.

"Oh—hi," he said. "I didn't notice any light, so I didn't ring."

"Duke," Peggy said, "this is Detective John Fanson. We work together."

"Hi." Her brother waved a casual greeting.

"We were having sandwiches. Do you want a sandwich?"

"I scoffed back already. I dig I better just fall out."

"I think it's time I left," John said. "I didn't realize how late it was."

"You cuttin', Jack?" Duke said. "Don't let me drag. I'm just here to hit a brace of the snowy whites."

"Yeah," John Fanson said, "I guess I'll cut." He looked at Duke with quiet interest. "I'm late for a date at a real gone pad; if I fluff with the stuff, they'll come on real sad."

Duke stiffened slightly, hesitated, and then said,

"Well, it was real nice to meet you, Mister Fanson. Good night, now. Good night, Peggy."

He left them, going down the hall to his bedroom. Peggy saw John to the door only moments later. He kissed her when he left, and there was a feeling of constraint and embarrassment evident to both of them as he did so.

And the next day she arrested Duke.

Woody and Duke had been at the flat before she returned from the ballet with John. She had known that, because there were the usual coffee cups and the uncleaned pot waiting in the sink for her. But it was not until John had left and she had gone into the kitchen to clean up that she noticed the envelope on the floor. It was partially wedged between a chair leg and the baseboard, as though it might have slipped from the pocket of a coat carelessly thrown over the chair back. It was unsealed and unaddressed, and of course she looked into it to see what it contained. In it was one typewritten page—a letter without date or signature:

> *Dear Joe,*
>
> *Your beef about the Buick sure gave me a laugh. So it had a cracked block, what do you expect a 90 day guarantee right from the factory? Maybe we should take it back and complain to the owner (ha ha). If the boys at the shop had seen it they would have welded it right then, but they are too busy to do engine jobs beside every thing else. By the time they change the serial nos., slip covers, do the paint job, and every thing they do not have time to do engine jobs as you can see. Besides, you can't just hire any one for the shop you can't be too careful. Frenchy has another mechanic lined up but I want to find out more about him first. So far no trouble and don't want any. Knock on wood but take your hat off first (ha ha). So it isn't any use to grip about the shop, every thing is all right up here. About the paint jobs, Frenchy says the air compressor was n.g. He got a new pump and things out to be ok.*

It sure gives me a laugh, you grip about things and then don't send the plates back on time, then we have to hold cars a week waiting. You will have to send the plates sooner. I keep my part of the bargain and I guess you can afford the expense (ha ha). I have found an other place to live, the landlady was too nosey, so now send everything to 668 Oak Street, Apt. 3–D. It is three flights, but I have four rooms. Crazy, man. There was one right below, but only two rooms.

Every thing is ok. The kids are not hip the cars don't all get left on the street where they drive them. Some dopes, how square can you get? It is worth all it costs to keep them going, so stop belly aching. I have to take the rap if if I get pulled in, and if the fuzz thinks it is just a 2 bit nuisance racket I won't get hit with a heavy rap. Once was enough.

Speaking of cops, I told you Dukes sister is a cop, but he is strictly ok. I want to fix it to give him a better deal and will write you about that when I get it worked out. Beside it is a good idea to have a direct line on what gives at head-quarters. If they get nosey we will know in time to pull out fast. Don't get any funny ideas. About the sister and I.

I guess that is enough for now. Don't forget to send the plates to the new address.

W.

She read the letter through quickly, then read it again more slowly. For several minutes after that she sat at the kitchen table with the paper before her and stared at it while she tried to consider what to do. Finally she got pen and paper and made a copy, and when that was done she put the letter back in its envelope and replaced it where she had found it. After that she finished the dishes and went to bed. In the morning, when she got up, Duke had already left the house and the letter was gone.

Her first move was to call in and ask for sick leave for the day. Then she left the house and took a bus to Oak Street. There was a chance that by going to the address she might run into Woody, and she wasn't ready for that yet, but it seemed likely that he would be out somewhere with Duke.

The superintendent of the building was a man in his late fifties who acted as though he had long ago encountered every situation which could possibly occur in his job and had found each one of them overwhelmingly dull. He managed to shake off enough of his lethargy, however, to admit that there was an apartment for rent.

Two rooms furnished.

"Second floor," he said. "They advertising that again?"

"I'd like to see it, please."

He sighed at that, but he tiredly led her up the stairs and, after some fumbling with a ring of keys, into the apartment.

"It's just as you see it," he told her. "No papering or painting, no alterations."

All but one window of the place faced on the blank wall of the adjoining building, and even at that hour of the day it was dark and gloomy. It was no place which Peggy would ever have chosen to live in, but that was of no consequence. Still, she made a pretence of inspecting it.

"What about the neighbors?" she asked, eyeing the ceiling. "Are there children upstairs?"

"No kids in the building. Fellow lives alone up there, just moved in. Looked quiet enough to suit me."

Peggy's shock at the rental price did not have to be feigned.

"That's rather high, isn't it?"

"Yep. So's everything today. That's what they're getting."

"Well ... I've got to live some place ..."

"Yep."

"I'll take it."

They were on the ground floor again when she suddenly said, "Oh dear, I've done it again! I left my purse on a chair up there." And, as he turned resignedly to go back, "No, don't bother. If you'll show me the right key I'll run up for it while you're getting the papers ready."

She had her hand out expectantly, and he did not hesitate to turn the key ring over to her. Again she climbed the stairs. Once inside the apartment, she made immediately for the bathroom, where she had noticed a bar of soap left by a previous tenant. She moistened the soap, flicked through the remaining keys until she found the one marked with Woody's apartment number, and pressed it as hard as she could against the softened bar. She wiped the key with a tissue, and with another she wrapped the soap, which she dropped into her purse.

When she returned the keys a few minutes later, and the super-intendent was making out a receipt for the rent, the man said,

"There's still a phone in that apartment. You want it connected?"

She hesitated. She had no idea of how much time she would be able to spend there, nor of how long it would take her to accomplish what she was engaged upon.

"I—yes, but not immediately. I'll get in touch with the company myself."

"How about the window washer? Want me to get hold of him?"

"Yes. Oh—wait. No, I'll do that myself." She had remembered the fire escape on the side of the building facing the blank wall. Her plans, only nebulous possibilities when she had arrived, were beginning to take form.

But when she left, something happened which made it appear that she was never going to use that apartment or the name "Margaret Starr" under which she had rented it.

CHAPTER SEVENTEEN
THE ARREST

S HE started for home, intending to pack a small bag with a few clothes and personal necessities which she would need at the new apartment. But on the way, a few blocks from her home, she left the bus and entered the cubby-hole key shop of a man who had been a neighbor for several years. She found him poring over a much-thumbed copy of a Dostoivesky novel. He was obviously pleased to see her; he and Mike, she remembered, had enjoyed an occasional game of chess together.

"Jake," she said, when they had passed the time of day, "I've got a rather special job here. Can you make a key from an impression?"

"Just an impression? You don't have the key itself?"

"That's right." She showed him the bar of soap. He studied it carefully over the tops of his steel-rimmed glasses.

"I guess I could, maybe. I wouldn't give any guarantee. But this is a funny job, Miss Malone. A key from an impression— that sounds like some kind of shenanigans, the sort of thing I wouldn't want to get mixed up with."

"It's police business, Jake."

"So?" He looked shrewdly at her. "Then why not have the work done at the police laboratory, where they understand such things?"

"I can't explain now. But look, Jake, you knew my father for a long time."

"Yes."

"And you know I'm on the force now. Everybody in the neighborhood knows it."

"I've heard that."

"Do you think I'm going to rob some place, then? That I don't have a really good reason for this, even if I can't tell you what it is?"

"All right," he sighed. "I'll see what I can do. Come back this afternoon. But remember—no guarantee."

"You're sweet, Jake. Maybe I'll be able to tell you soon what I want it for."

"I'm not so sure I want to know," he grumbled gruffly.

At the door of the shop she paused with one hand on the knob.

"Jake, have you made any keys for my brother lately?"

"Duke? No. I don't see him much nowadays. Should I be making keys for him?"

"He said something about losing his key ring. I guess he must have found it." She went out, leaving the old man studying the bar of soap.

She had scarcely turned the corner toward her own street when she saw Duke. He was just getting out of Woody's car, which had pulled up a few yards from the intersection. As she stopped to watch, Woody's car shot ahead, and Duke walked to a car which was parked at the curb and began to do something to the door lock. He seemed to have trouble with it at first, but soon the door swung open and he got in. There was another delay while, sitting behind the wheel, he appeared to be busy with something under the dashboard. Then the engine came to life, he twisted the wheel, and the car moved out into traffic.

She had no time for thought. Dodging a car coming from the other direction, she ran across the street directly in front of the one Duke was driving. He pulled up short with a squeal of brakes, and she was around the side and had the door open before the fenders had stopped rocking.

"What the hell—" Duke began. Then, "Oh, it's you. What's the matter? You crazy or something?"

"What are you doing in this car?" Peggy demanded.

"Minding my own business. Close the door; you're making a draft."

"Pull it back."

"What? You gone nuts? Look, I'm in a hurry. You got something on your mind, I'll see you at the house tonight. Or leave me a note."

"I want you to repark this car and get out. That's an order."

"An order? Look, big stuff, you're not giving orders to baby brother any more. I pay my way. If you want an argument, I'll see you tonight. I don't have time now."

"I'm not speaking as your sister. Back this car to the curb. That's a police order. I'm serious, Duke."

"Jeee—sus! So I didn't put out my hand when I pulled away—nothing was coming anyway."

"It's more serious than that. Park it."

He reluctantly returned the car to its original place. Once it was parked, he appeared anxious to leave it.

"All right," he said, "you want to talk to me, let's go somewhere and talk." He reached under the dashboard, the motor died, and he quickly slipped something into his pocket.

"I think we can talk right here," Peggy said. "This isn't your car, is it?"

"What do you care? Let's not sit here all day."

"Whose car is it, Duke?"

"What does that matter? I've got a license to drive."

"But do you have the owner's permission to drive *this* car? Let's go and ask him."

"Hey, look, this is a free country! You can't just go around sticking your nose in where it doesn't belong!"

"Let's talk to the owner, Duke. Do you know who he is?"

"That goddamn badge sure has swelled your head. Suppose I just tell you to go to hell?"

"Then I guess we'll have to make a trip downtown. First of all, though, I want to see what you just put into your pocket."

"And what if I won't show you?"

"I'll know, eventually. You're not talking to your sister now. You're talking to a cop. I know how to get help if I need it. Don't make it any harder on yourself."

"You mean you're going to pinch me? Your own brother? Some big fat deal! Only, on what charge?"

"Suspicion, if nothing else. Let's see it, Duke. The pocket."

Not waiting for him to comply, she shoved her hand into his jacket and drew out a piece of taped wire with two alligatorclip ends.

"What is this?"

"Part of a radio. I'm building a crystal set to put in my hat when I eat enough corn flakes to get my Junior G-Man badge."

"All right, wise guy. I know an ignition jumper when I see one."

She walked to the back of the car and copied down the license number. Then she hailed a passing cab.

"Precinct house," she said to the driver, as she held the door open for Duke to get in.

"Name?"

"Girard Malone."

The desk sergeant's eyebrows lifted as he made a notation on the page.

"What charge, officer?"

"Attempted theft of an automobile."

"Owner's complaint?"

"No. My complaint."

"Name of the owner."

"I don't know. I have the license number."

The officer at the desk looked doubtful, marked down the number she gave him, and then called across the room,

"Pulaski!"

"Yes, sir?"

"Take this fellow aside for a minute. Don't lock him up yet. I want to speak to Officer Malone."

"Yes, sir!"

When Duke had been led away, the sergeant leaned over the desk and said,

"What the hell is this all about, anyway?"

"It's an arrest. I want the boy booked."

"You haven't been on the force very long, have you?"

"No."

"Well, I don't want to see you make a mistake. What were the circumstances leading up to the arrest?"

"I observed him entering a car and attempting to drive it away."

"And then you arrested him?"

"Yes."

"For God's sake, why? Someone gets into a car and starts off. You arrest him. You don't have the owner here as complainant—you don't even know who the owner is. Maybe this fellow owns the car, for all I can see."

"He doesn't own it. I know that."

"How do you know it?"

"He's my brother."

"Your—I thought it was a funny coincidence about the name, but I didn't want to say anything."

"He's my brother, and I know he had no right to be in that car. He started it with a circuit jumper. I saw the whole thing."

"This must be Duke, then. Your father was always talking about his kids."

"Yes, that's Duke."

"And you want him booked? I mean, you couldn't—well, straighten it out somehow? Between you and him, and maybe the owner of the car?"

"This is an arrest. Let's get it over with."

"All right, Malone. It's crazy, but I guess you're just as stubborn as your father. Pulaski! Bring that fellow back here!"

Duke was sneeringly resentful. He answered the questions concerning his age and address as though they were outrageous intrusions upon his rights and privacy.

"I want to make a phone call," he insisted. "I have that much coming to me in this deal, haven't I? You can't just pull anybody in off the street and lock them up without anyone knowing where they are or what's happened to them."

The sergeant shoved the phone toward him.

"Make your call, buster."

"Jeeze, thanks," Duke said sarcastically. As he lifted the instrument from its cradle, he asked, "Does she have to be in on this?"

"This isn't a private, privileged communication, son. If you have a lawyer and he comes to see you, that's different."

Duke viciously hooked the dial, turning so that Peggy could not observe the number he called, and coughing ostentatiously to make it impossible for her to count the clicks. After a few moments he said,

"Pete? Look, get hold of Woody, fast. I been hooked. Yeah ... yeah, that's right. Twelfth Precinct. Yeah ... yeah. No, my sist— he'll find out when he gets here. Look, don't take a slow boat to China on the way. You can get crummy in half an hour in one of these joints."

He tossed the phone back on its cradle and shoved it contemptuously back at the desk sergeant.

"All right," he said to Peggy. "Have me locked up now. But just see how long I stay."

"Take him away, Pulaski," said the sergeant. He looked at Peggy and shook his head.

"Stick around," Duke said over his shoulder. "You won't have long to wait."

"I might do that," Peggy replied.

The desk sergeant shook his head.

CHAPTER EIGHTEEN
PASS KEY

I T WAS less than half an hour later when Woody appeared, and with him was an older man, a stranger. Woody did most of the talking; when the other man spoke he was either agreeing with, or amplifying, something Woody had said. It appeared that there had been a ridiculous mistake on the part of the police—and wasn't this a free country any more? The man was the owner of the car in which Duke had been picked up, and he carried papers to prove it. He had asked Duke to drive his car to a nearby garage for a grease job, and he was annoyed at having been called away from his printing shop by all this nonsense.

"He was taking this car with your knowledge, then?" the desk sergeant asked.

"Sure it was with my knowledge. I gave him half a buck to take the heap down to Ajax. Next thing I hear some dopey cop has him down here and my car is still where it was, no grease job."

The sergeant fiddled with his pen and turned to Peggy.

"You suppose there's the possibility of a mistake here, Officer Malone?"

Peggy was stunned, then angry. She turned from Woody's smirk to the nervous frown of the car's owner.

"What time did you give him the keys?"

"I don't know, exactly. Maybe ten, ten-thirty. What does that matter?"

"But you did give them to him? You remember giving him the keys?"

"Sure, I told you. I gave him half a buck to—say, do I have to go all over that again? Isn't it enough that I have to leave the shop and come down here?"

"If you gave him the car keys," Peggy said, "how does it happen that he was using this to start the engine?"

She shook the circuit jumper in the man's face, and he moved back a startled step or two, looking at Woody.

"He didn't mean he gave him keys, exactly," Woody said. "He meant he gave him what he always uses to start the car. He lost his keys, so he uses that thing there."

"Let the man speak for himself," Peggy snapped. Then, to the printer, "Do you mean to tell me that you always go to the trouble of hooking up this wire when you want to go somewhere?"

"I guess it's my own business how I start my car, lady. There's no law says I can't start it that way, is there? I lost my keys, so I use that thing."

"You always use it?"

"I—yes. Sure."

"How do you use it?" She held the wire behind her. "Describe this article. How is it constructed?"

"Why, you take it and—and, well, you fasten it to the ignition and … uh …"

"Just a second," Woody interrupted. "This man owns an automobile, and he's proved that. This—officer—says her brother stole it, and he says it never was stolen. I don't see how it figures that he has to give any explanations about how he takes care of the car or if he keeps his road maps under the seat instead of in the glove compartment. That's his business. If there's any explaining to be done, I think it ought to be done from the other end, by this—officer—here. What kind of a case is this? Who is being charged, and what are they being charged with?"

"Pulaski!" shouted the sergeant. "That kid in Section A—turn him out."

"Yes, *sir!*"

Peggy's fists clenched until her nails bit into her palms.

"Are you countermanding this arrest, Sergeant?"

"I am, Malone. I don't want you to make any more a damn fool of yourself than you already have. You just don't have a charge. I don't see why you brought the lad here in the first place."

"I can tell you," Woody interjected. "It's just a family affair. They had an argument, so she takes it out on him by trying to arrest him. A fine way for a cop to use the badge, if you ask me."

"You shut up too!" the sergeant barked. "You talk a little too smart to suit me. There's something funny about the whole thing, and maybe it's just luck that you're not up here yourself."

"There's something funny, all right," Peggy said. "I'd like to see this man pick Duke out of a line-up. I'd be willing to bet my badge that he doesn't even know him."

"Officer Malone, you very nearly have bet your badge already—and lost it. If I were you, I wouldn't say any more."

"I just came here," put in the printer, "to say nobody stole my car and to get that boy out of trouble. The way *she* acts, I'm in trouble for doing that. What is this—Russia?"

"All right. All *right!*" the desk sergeant said desperately.

Duke appeared just then. He waved a hand at Woody and managed to include the printer in his grin of greeting.

"Is this the fellow," asked the sergeant, "who you gave the key—the—Oh, to hell with it!"

"Sure it's him. That fellow right there. Uh ... Duke."

"Lucky thing for you you're my sister," Duke said to Peggy. "Boy, could I slap you down with a suit for false arrest!"

"That's something else," Woody spoke up. "Does this go down on the books against him as a pinch?"

"So far as I'm concerned," the sergeant said, "there never was any arrest. Officer Malone and her brother just stopped by for a social call. And now if everybody is satisfied," he said, "will you please all clear the hell out?"

Peggy remained behind as the others left, Duke jauntily leading the way. She looked at the wire she still held, then dropped it into the wastebasket also.

"What a rig-job," she said bitterly. "I wonder how much Woody paid that man to buy him off? Plenty. It must have been plenty."

"Malone," said the sergeant, "just what the devil were you trying to do? Is this really a family affair, or are you working under orders? Because you sure made a hell of a mess out of it."

"Call it a family affair for now," Peggy said. She moved aside, picking up her purse as a uniformed patrolman walked in with a blowzy, middle-aged woman who was arguing in the cackling tones of a ruffled hen.

"By the way," the sergeant remarked as he automatically reached for his pen, "I thought you were off sick today."

"I am sick," Peggy said. "I'm getting sicker by the minute."

When Peggy returned to the apartment on Oak Street she brought with her two suitcases and a dubious key to Woody's apartment upstairs. She was in a mood of wavering indecision as to whether or not she should move out of the old flat entirely, leaving it to Duke. After what had happened, it was going to be anything but easy for them to live together. On the other hand, he must not know that she had moved into Woody's building. It might be possible, of course, to give him her new phone number and no address, so that he could get in touch with her if he had to, if he got into a jam that Woody couldn't fix. But Woody was a pretty good fixer, as she had learned at her own expense. She wished that Tom would get back from his trip to Washington; she needed advice badly.

With her bags unpacked, she left to buy a few groceries and other household necessities. While she was out she called the telephone company's service department and arranged to have the phone connected next day. It was mid-afternoon when she changed into a pair of old, paint-spattered dungarees, tied a kerchief over her head, and started washing the windows.

In itself, the task was pointless. Grimy or clean, those windows would never admit enough light to dispel the gloom. But Peggy had other reasons for doing the job.

Two of her windows faced on the landing of the fire escape. Standing out there with her bucket of water, her sponges and chamois, she had an opportunity to study the windows of the apartment above.

Woody was not in. She was almost positive of that, for she had listened carefully for the least sound, sitting in frozen silence for long moments. But she was afraid to go up and try her key at his door; she did not know his habits well enough to risk having him surprise her. And so she washed her windows and washed them again, gathering her courage for the next step.

From the window above her, a loose piece of insulated wire dangled, flapping against the brick side of the building with every breeze. It was, apparently, one of those mysterious odds and ends left over from a previous tenancy, the purpose of which is never quite clear, and which later occupants never get around to discarding. It could have been the broken lead-in from a long-discarded radio antenna; it could have been a number of things. The loose end hung just above the top of her own windows.

Fifteen minutes on the fire escape assured her that whatever she did now was unlikely to be observed. The opposite wall was entirely blank; from the street, a passerby might have glanced up into that cul-de-sac and only noticed a woman doing some outside household chore. So she took her pail and sponges and climbed up one flight of the iron framework. And there, under pretense of being busy with the window, she made a quick survey of what she could see of Woody's apartment.

It was furnished with the same type of rickety cast-offs as her own, all scarred and marked with the cynical, almost deliberate abuse of two decades. On a desk, the open pigeonholes of which were untidily crammed with envelopes and papers, was a battered portable typewriter. A rack beside a chair overflowed with newspapers and garish magazines. On a table there was a small radio. The loose wire which Peggy had noticed obviously had no present use; it ran under the window sash in a sort of slot which had been bored, or gouged out, many years before, and came to its purposeless end behind the radiator directly beneath the window. So much for the living room.

At the other end of the iron fire escape was one of the bedroom's two windows. Aside from the fact that the bed was made, which rather surprised her, Peggy found nothing of any interest there. After a few moments' inspection, she took her pail and made her way back to her own apartment.

Later she went to a radio store where she rented a tape recorder, selecting a model which would operate for two hours without attention, and asking a great many questions about extending the microphone lead wire. At her request, and for an additional charge, a young man from the shop delivered the machine and set it up. After he had left, she spent an hour or so in experimenting with it. Satisfied, finally, that she thoroughly understood its operation, she put it out of sight in a closet. Then she returned to the flat, mentally preparing herself for the scene she anticipated when she would see her brother.

CHAPTER NINETEEN
ECSTASY

SHE PREPARED A MEAL FOR TWO, then ate alone, for Duke did not come home. He did not come home for dinner and he was not home at eight o'clock, when the phone rang.

Tom was on the wire, calling from Washington.

"Tom!" Peggy exclaimed when she heard his voice. "I'm so glad you called!"

"You sound upset. Has something happened?"

"Everything has happened. Tom, I arrested Duke today."

"Arrested Duke! Good Lord! Why?"

"I caught him stealing a car. I know he was stealing it. But half an hour after I took him in, Woody Russell was at the station house with the owner of the car. The owner wouldn't press charges. In fact ..."

And she went on to describe the whole incident, beginning at the point where she had seen Duke trying to start the car. Tom listened carefully, occasionally interjecting a pointed question.

"I guess it's time," Tom said when she had finished, "to get that boy in line. I hoped it wouldn't be necessary to get tough with him. Since things have gone this far—well, I'm afraid we'll just have to show him where he heads in."

Peggy had not yet mentioned the apartment she had rented that day. She started to speak of it now, then decided not to; Tom might consider her attempt to gather evidence against Woody as a childish game of cops-and-robbers. But she read him the copy of the letter she had found.

"You can see what he's doing," she said when she had finished. "Those kids think they're just giving somebody a hard time when they drive a car off. Actually, he's using them as stooges in the first stage of these thefts, the most dangerous part. After they've taken a car out of its neighborhood, someone else picks it up without much risk. Then it goes through the plant and comes out looking like an entirely different car. After that it's driven to this fellow Joe, who takes over from there. From what I know of Woody, I'd say that Joe, whoever that is, probably lives in New Orleans. Maybe he's a used-car dealer. Anyway, New Orleans is a port city, and right now there's a big market for good cars in South America."

"You think Duke is helping steal cars which end up in Argentina?" Tom laughed. "That sounds rather far-fetched, doesn't it?"

"Tom, those cars are going somewhere. I've been checking the record books lately. You haven't any idea of the car-theft situation in this city. It's terrific. But what happens to the cars isn't important, so far as Duke is concerned. All I want is to get him out of this mess before he's in so deep that we can't pull him out."

"We'll get him out," Tom promised. "We'll get him out so fast that his head will spin. And then we'll see what's to be done about this Woody fellow. But that will have to wait for another couple of days. The reason I phoned was to tell you that I wouldn't be back as soon as I expected to be. I'll be detained here for two more days, maybe three."

"Oh."

"But don't worry. Just don't push things until I get back. Whatever Duke is mixed up in now hasn't happened overnight. The situation won't change overnight, either. Take things easy until I see you and we have a chance to really talk this over."

"You mean I mustn't arrest him again, is that it?" Peggy said with a tinge of annoyed sarcasm. It was easy, she thought, for Tom to point out her mistake after she had made it, to subtly criticize an action undertaken in the stress of blind excitement.

"Well," Tom said, "you didn't get very far the first time, did you?"

"All right, boss, I won't do a thing until you say it's all right. Is that what you want?"

"Peg, what is wrong with you? I'm not talking just because I like the sound of my own voice. I'm trying to tell you what I think is the best way of handling this thing. I can't do anything until I get back. In the meantime, if you insist on going off half-cocked, I will understand why. You can be sure of my sympathy, if not my approval. Do whatever you think you have to do, but don't expect me to stand up and cheer if you flub it."

"I'm sorry, Tom," she said. Anger had died, if the undertone of resentment still remained. "You're right. I know you're right. I'll do as you say."

"I'll see you soon. Don't worry. I'll take care of this."

"Yes, Tom."

"Try to think of it as my problem, rather than yours. There shouldn't be any problems for you to shoulder now."

"All right, Tom. I'll do whatever you say."

"You don't have to bother yourself with it any longer."

"Whatever you say. I'll do what you want."

"Just wait. Let me take care of it."

"I'll do whatever you say, darling," she said.

And then the connection was broken.

Duke still had not returned when, half an hour later, she received another phone call—this one from John Fanson.

"I have a new toy," he said. "I'm looking for someone to help me play with it."

"A cat?" she hazarded.

"I already have a cat. I suppose this really isn't as entertaining as a cat. Today I finally broke down and bought a television set."

"Oh Lord!" she exclaimed. "Murder plays, Arthur Godfrey, boxing, Arthur Godfrey, ancient movies, Arthur Godfrey, comics, Arthur Godfrey—thanks, but I've already seen television."

"But how about the first performance of a new Menotti opera? Starts in half an hour."

"Bang-bang," she said. "I was working the d.w. out of h.q., when we got a p.d.q. on the seven-oh-seven. The m.o. checked with an i.d. we had filed in Section Six, so I put on a general alert. It figured."

"Laughton's reading tonight, too," he went on unperturbedly. "A bit precious, perhaps, but shall I come over now and pick you up?"

"In ten minutes."

While she waited for John, Peggy wrote a note for her brother:

Duke—

After today's bust, I'm not sure we want to continue to put up with each other's company. I won't be home tonight. I'll let you know in a couple of days what plans I've made for the future.

She was wise enough to stop at that point and sign it. A dozen bitter, recriminatory phrases rushed to mind, but she refused to allow anger to trap her. When the bell rang, announcing John's arrival, the message waited on a table where Duke could not fail to find it.

In accepting John's invitation, Peggy had planned to stay for an hour or so, then take a cab to her new place on Oak Street.

Somehow, though, things did not work out that way. In the first place, she discovered that beer and pretzels went well with Menotti, provided one did not crunch at the wrong times. And John's couch was very comfortable.

She had wondered how he lived. What she saw now bore out what she had vaguely imagined and conjectured from what she knew of him.

His apartment was not large, but one had no sense of being cramped in it. There was a feeling of adequate space in which to pace about; she was sure that, if two people occupied it, they would each be afforded that most important, if seldom mentioned, luxury—a door of one's own to slam. The most striking feature was the number of books. Books lined the walls from floor to ceiling in every room. They overflowed the shelving, spilled across window sills, crouched in odd corners of space, and their subject matter covered everything from the mores of the ancient Egyptians, as described by Wilkinson, to the idiosyncracies of Bryn Mawr as discerned by Kinsey. Where there were not books there were phonograph records, ranging from the early, untutored washboard-thumpings of Baby Dodds to the sophisticated bangings of the latter-day saints of modern symphony. The available wall space remaining was taken up by reproductions of the works of famous painters and by carefully framed etchings, photographs and drawings arranged in such apparently haphazard fashion that Rembrandt's *Death of the Virgin* was juxtaposed with an original panel from a comic strip. Much of the furniture, she saw, had either been made by John or adapted by him to some other purpose than was originally intended.

It was an interesting, casual, relaxing place. Too much so, perhaps, she began to think. The idea of returning to the dismal barrenness of the Oak Street apartment became less and less attractive as time went by. She liked being where she was; she felt at home here.

During an interlude which would normally have been given over to advertising the sponsor's product, but which, because this was a highly cultural program, was now taken up by an announcer's explanation of why there would be no advertising of the sponsor's product, John selected one of several crusty old pipes from a rack on the mantel. Tamping it to the brim with an apple-mellowed shag cut, he rummaged fruitlessly in his pockets for a match.

"Let me light it," Peggy offered. For an instant, as he bent to receive the flame, she recalled that this had been a ritual of her childhood, an important, grave ceremony shared with Big Mike.

It should not have been a surprise to her, what happened later. It took some time, but it happened. And she had not even the excuse of intoxication—any form of intoxication—this time. She was stone-cold sober when John's hand fell upon her knee; she was still sober when it slipped under her skirt and up her thigh.

It had never occurred to her, in accepting John's invitation, that the possibility of physical infidelity to Tom was inherent in the situation. But, somehow, things happened. And then she was naked on the little heap of her own clothing before the couch. The deep pile of the loop rug was soft under her knees. And John's pipe had gone out.

"Let me light it."

She found matches and reached up to rekindle the glow. Then, furtively glancing up at him as he concerned himself with the pipe's burblings, she proceeded to consummate at great length, and with many side excursions, her infidelity.

Of course she stayed the night. Before the night was over, Tom Flanagan's cuckoldry was affirmed and reaffirmed without any possible question of doubt. She felt guilty about that at first, and then she felt defiant, and of her defiance was bred, of course, excess. It was not enough that John must use her as Tom had; he must go further, even when she had to indicate the way. And so she exhausted both of them.

But one thing she learned that night. It was not only Tom Flanagan who could lead her to ecstasy.

CHAPTER TWENTY
WIRE TRAP

"A LINE TAP, LADY? Jeezus, no! It's worth my job. You can't just tie in on somebody else's phone. They got laws about that. It's illegal. You know. You can't do it. You ain't supposed to."

The man who had come to connect her phone scratched his ear as she laid a ten-dollar bill on the table and ironed out its creases with her thumb.

"I can't do it, lady."

She put a second bill on top of the first.

"Look," he said, "it won't do you no good. You can keep piling those bills up all you want to—the answer is still no. You wouldn't want somebody listening in on *your* phone, would you?"

"But you do know how to do it? It isn't a big, complicated job, is it?"

"Sure I know how to do it. There's half a dozen ways. Only I'm not going to. Jeeze, if you got trouble with your neighbors, lady, that's one thing. Only, listening in on their phone, that's going too far. I got orders to connect a phone, I connect a phone. That's all I'm here for."

Peggy flipped open her wallet and laid it on the table. The gold shield spoke for her, now.

"Jeeze," the man said after a pause during which he studied the badge from the corner of his eye. "Jeeze, I don't know. I never ran into anything like this before. Lots of nuts, sure, but nothing

like this. If this is a police job, why don't they call in to the office
and clear it with somebody there? Just give me my orders and I
do the job, like I'm supposed to? I don't have any authority to go
ahead on my own, police or no police. It seems funny any way
you look at it, if you ask me. Why didn't they call in to the office?"

"Maybe," Peggy said, "the office would rather not know anything about it. Officially, that is. How long have you been with
the company now?"

"Three years, but I never—"

"All right. Then you ought to know by now that the office
never issues an order for a wire-tap. They may know about it, but
they've got to look the other way. What's your name, again?"

"Hekborne. Bill Hekborne. Only I don't see—"

"That's right," Peggy nodded, as though his name had been
known to her for some time. "And why do you think, Bill, that
you were sent out on this particular job?"

"Well, it's part of my section. There are three of us take care
of anything from Hortley Street down to the park."

"But they picked you for this one. Because they know you're
reliable; your record has held up under investigation. They know
you're close-mouthed, and don't tell all you know. Not like some
people, who start blabbing as soon as they've had a couple of
beers."

"Maybe I ought to call in. If I get an okay from Mister Birch,
that's different. I can't go ahead on my own."

"Old pussyfoot," Peggy said, assuming that the nomencla-
ture of business offices was universal, or at least standardized,
"won't give you an okay. He can't. If you talk to him, he'll act as
though he didn't know what it was all about. He's depending on
you to handle this by yourself. In fact, the whole thing is over his
head—a long way over his head."

"Gosh, I don't know. If I do a job like that—well, I've got my own style, like. Like a painter, sort of. The way I make a bind, and all. Anybody who knows the way I work would know who did it."

"Then you won't work in your own style. You'll make it look as though some amateur did the job. As though I did it."

He considered this possibility.

"I wouldn't want to use company material. Their wire is all coded."

"I have a lamp extension cord we can cut up."

"How about tape? Theirs is all marked, see? It spells out, 'I believe that I receive a very adequate wage', every twelve inches. That way you always know how much you're using."

"Would adhesive tape be all right?"

"That's a good idea," he said. "That's just what some amateur might use."

"We're in business," Peggy said.

"You want it so it rings your phone when they get a call, is that it? You don't want just a dead cut-in?"

"All I need," Peggy told him, "is an old-fashioned party-line set-up. Is that a lost art?"

"Well, you don't want them answering your calls, do you? You want to listen to them or you want them to listen to you? I can fix it however you say."

They discussed the various possibilities for a few minutes, after which the man left the apartment for the subterranean mysteries of the cellar. Twenty minutes later he returned, and after some further work on Peggy's phone he announced that the operation was concluded. A soft buzz would now alert her to any call which Woody might receive, at which time she could listen in simply by picking up her own phone. Messages on her line were inviolate.

"When it's a case of law and order," he said, pocketing the twenty dollars she had laid out, "I guess you can forget about a regulation or two. Right is right, the way I see it. We got too many laws now, saying what you can't do. This is a free country, isn't it?"

"The door," she told him, "sticks. You have to lift it to make sure it latches when you leave."

This was in mid-morning. Waking early, she had crept quietly from John Fanson's bed, had let herself out of his apartment, had eaten a soda-counter breakfast. Calling the precinct house, she had asked for a week's extension of sick-leave. That much time, she hoped, would be plenty for her purpose. If not—well, the future would take care of itself.

After the telephone man had left, she allowed herself a few moments of relaxation on the narrow, sharp-edged day bed inadequately disguised as a couch. She had to collect her thoughts, get her plans, if she really had plans, into some semblance of order.

She could not—she dared not—now think of what had happened between her and John Fanson, and what it meant in her relationship to Tom. That was something to think about later. She had been unfaithful to the man who was practically her husband. Very well—so she had been unfaithful. She had acted the bitch. Very well. Very well indeed, now that she gave it a moment's consideration. But she could not worry about that now. Tomorrow, or the day after tomorrow. That was when one thought about one's personal lapses, wasn't it? Today she had to put her mind to the solution of the problem which Duke had brought upon her.

The solution, of course, was to put Woody behind bars, where he belonged. To do that, she had to have admissible evidence of what he was doing. The letter she had copied meant nothing, so far as that went, even though it told an almost complete story of his operations. And anything she might pick up through tapping his telephone would be, in itself, unacceptable. What she had to do was learn as much about his associates as she could, know who came to his apartment, who called him, what they talked about. Given time, she could build a case around him that couldn't be beaten or bought off.

What she had to do now was put the tape recorder to work at the job for which she had rented it. And she was nervous. Woody was not at home. But he might return at any moment; she really knew very little about his habits. There was the superintendent to consider, and the neighbors. And what would happen if some cleaning woman, for instance, noticed signs of her tampering with the wire behind Woody's radiator and brought it to his attention? How dangerous a man was he? What might he do if he found her spying upon him?

There was also the possibility that the key Jake had made for her would not even open Woody's door ...

She was afraid to go up to his apartment. She recognized that, admitted it to herself, and was conscious that she was deliberately putting it off. But it had to be done some time, and so finally she forced herself to abandon her so-called planning and do something concrete.

The first thing she did was connect the recorder to the wire which dangled from the window above. She managed to waste some time concealing the lead wire which ran under the carpet from her window to the closet where the machine was, but finally this was completed. Into a paper bag she put the microphone, a pair of wire-cutting pliers, two screwdrivers, tape, and a length of wire. And then, with what she hoped was the proper combination of stealth and assurance, she left her gloomy little hole-in-the-wall and went upstairs.

Jake's key fitted perfectly.

CHAPTER TWENTY-ONE
DIG THAT JIVE

THE radiator had a cover—a shell of light metal perforated to give the effect of a basket weave—and this fact gave Peggy some assurance that her intrusion might remain unnoticed indefinitely. There was ample room under the shell to accommodate the microphone, and it was also possible to arrange it in such a way that no wiring was visible. She made the necessary connection, taped the bare copper, and fought back an impulse to immediately rush out of the place.

Downstairs, she had left the recording machine on, the tape slowly threading through the magnetizing head. Its controls were set so that any sound she now made should not only be recorded, but should at the same time be quietly amplified through the speaker.

"One-two-three-four," she said. "Testing."

That was what they always said, wasn't it?

"One-two-three-four." Softer, this time, and at the other side of the room. "Testing. Hello, hello, hello. C-Q, C-Q, C-Q. A tisket, a tasket, a green and yaller basket."

She giggled nervously.

"Say something, now," she said. "Keep talking, so you'll know if it works. My name is Margaret Malone. I think I am maybe a little bit crazy. I am twenty-odd years old. I am a bitch. I got awnts in my pense. Haunts in my pense. But I do promise to love, honor, and oh, baby!"

While she was talking she had walked into the bedroom and back again. Now she stopped at the desk on which Woody's typewriter sat, and thumbed through some of the pigeonholed papers.

"The boy stood on the burning deck, eating peanuts by the peck ..."

The papers were a disappointment. Either Woody destroyed his personal correspondence or he kept it elsewhere, and she did not feel up to making an extended search of the place. All she found was a collection of advertisements and a couple of small bills from neighborhood merchants.

"... combed his hair with a wagon wheel, and died with a toothpick in his heel. So, shoot, if you must, this old gray head, but spare your country's flag, she said. C-Q, C-Q ..."

She put the papers back as she had found them, picked up the few scraps of wire insulation and similar evidences of her visit. Satisfied, finally, that no incriminating trace of what she had been up to was left behind, she turned at the door and said to the empty room,

"I am not now, and never have been, a member of the human race."

Back in her own apartment, she went immediately to the recorder and changed its controls to play-back. There was a long period of meaningless howling, indicative of that extended time when the machine had been running but the circuit incomplete. Then, through a confusion of background noise, of paper-rustlings, and the apparently aimless movement of her footsteps, she heard, briefly, her own voice. The sound was murky and rasped like a long-disused and rusty file, but it could be heard and understood if one listened. After all, one did not expect high-fidelity on such equipment. It could be heard and understood, and she was somewhat amusedly embarrassed by what she had said, and she wasted no time in erasing it.

"Never said a mumblin' word," she murmured as she ran the tape back and reset the machine to record.

Woody's phone rang once during that afternoon. She did not respond to the quiet buzzing on her line which marked the call, for she knew that he was not in. Twice, when she heard footsteps going up the stairs past her apartment, she switched on the recorder. Both times, such was the sensitivity of the microphone, she was able to hear the steps go by his door, both in the loudspeaker and, later, by playing the tape. With nothing else to occupy her time, she cleaned the refrigerator and then the stove. After that she lay down and thought about John Fanson and Tom Flanagan and Jacques Dubois. She was tired in a way which quickly led her to a sort of hypnologic state rather than true sleep.

A long time later, she sat up, startled by that secretive, insinuating sound which indicated that someone was trying to call Woody. A quick glance at the clock told her that five hours had gone by.

She heard the heavy tap of heels overhead; the signal of her phone ceased, and she bounded across the room to take up the instrument.

Somebody named Juggy wanted to borrow twenty dollars. Woody said no. But there was a story that went with it. Woody did not want to hear the story. But there was also a blonde that maybe went with it. Woody hesitated here, then said no again, and after that he hung up. Peggy recorded the time of the call in a notebook, along with what had been said.

She turned on the tape recorder then. What she heard through the speaker was mostly the bang of shoes on bare floor, the rap of buttons as a jacket was thrown over a chair. Whistled fragments of tune accompanied Woody's activities, with an occasional, self-directed remark such as "Where did I put that damned cigarette?" Once there was a soft, not-quite-surprised, "hmmm ..." such as a man might make upon discovering that his watch had stopped or that the level of the whiskey bottle is low, and shortly after that he began to make preparations for a bath. She could clearly hear the water filling the tub, and about then Woody burst into song. He was obviously a bathroom baritone, and the song was ribald. She turned off the machine. After all, there were areas of Woody's life which had no bearing on what she was trying to find out about him; he was unlikely to discuss his business secrets with himself while bathing.

Later she heard him go out—for dinner, probably, for he was back within an hour. During that hour she made a meal for herself, and was settled down with a magazine when he returned. She turned the recorder on again.

She was getting used to that gadget now. With the speaker softly carrying the sounds of the apartment upstairs, it was almost as though one lived with another person in the house. She was becoming familiar with his habits—the mutter of occasional profanity, the absent-minded whistling of old New Orleans street-marches: *Didn't He Ramble*, for instance, or *Free As A Bird*. Time went by, and she found that she could read her magazine article and still be aware of what was going on in Woody's place. As a teacher, she had often wondered about the teen-ager's ability to study trigonometry while a radio blasted. Apparently the trick was not difficult; the human mind easily divided into sections, like an orange.

At seven-thirty Woody's phone rang, and she picked hers up carefully. It was Juggy, and the amount mentioned was now ten dollars. Also, the blonde had acquired a sister. The conversation was short, and the answer was still no. Afterward, Woody fulminated for at least ten minutes, while Peggy giggled at what came over the system.

Eight-ten went down in her notebook as the time when Duke called.

"That dopey sister of mine, man ..."

"Dig you, man ..."

"Hasn't fallen in yet. And won't be, dig? Gotta scratch my own scoff. Like to famish and perish in small, easy installments."

"Rough scuffle, man."

"Like it's not enough she comes on salty all the time, and I go into an Uncle Tom over the gold issue until I can put it out in front. Like she reaches out with the long arm for the big bust, only there's nothing to bust and I get a full shake instead. Like she hasn't been a full-time drag all around, and from Delaware all the way, *she* cuts out. She cuts, and I don't know from note one. What the hell laundry has my shirts, for instance? What goes?

"Play it cool, man. You're holding these days. If the cuffs get dirty, go out and lay a new one on yourself. Fifteen bucks, I know where you can get a real gone white-on-white."

"Solid, but how does *she* figure to cut? That's my burn."

"Took your chorus, man. You don't blow on time, somebody's on your note already. Dig it good. Hip yourself to something."

"Crazy. Only I can't ball with this kick. What laundry my shirts in?"

It took a great deal of self-control for Peggy not to interrupt to tell Duke that she had been doing the laundry herself and that his shirts were all in his bureau. She managed to remain silent, however, and after five minutes or so, Duke gave up complaining and hung up.

It was her turn to fume. She stamped about the apartment sucking a cigarette which refused to burn properly. Upstairs,

Woody became musical again, vocally punning for his own amusement. He wished he were in Dixie, because Dixie was a wonderful girl. A pretty girl was like a malady ...

She turned the recorder off, then turned it on again. And the telephone rang.

This time it was not Juggy. It was not even the blonde. It was not the blonde's sister, either. It was a friend of the blonde's sister, and there was mention of five dollars. Before Woody hung up, he had a question to ask:

"You got anything there for about a dollar ninety-eight? Now, of course I know you don't get the same quality in the ten-cent necktie that you get in the fifteen-cent necktie, but—"

The girl, being a respectable girl, proved it by cutting the connection first. And Peggy went back to her magazine, and for a time there was a vast, empty silence.

Nine o'clock.

She ran back the tape. What had been recorded wasn't worth keeping. Start over again.

Eight-twenty.

Nine-twenty-two.

Ten-twenty-four.

Woody had another call.

"Your name Russell? Woodrow Russell?"

"Something like that."

The voice on the other end of the line was strangely muffled. And it was a wholly unnatural voice. A man speaking in falsetto? A woman attempting to deepen the tone of her speech? Peggy knew only that an effort at disguise was being made.

"I'd like to talk to you."

"It's your dime. Say something."

"I don't mean over the phone."

"I can hear you. Say your algebra."

"I think we have something to discuss."

"I'm willin'."

"It's a business matter."

"What sort of business?"

"The automobile business."

A long wait, and then Woody said,

"What about the automobile business?"

"I think it could be better."

"I don't believe I know what you're talking about."

"I think you do. When can we get together?"

"Who am I talking to?" Woody asked.

The other voice laughed.

"Tell me more about the automobile business," Woody suggested.

"It could be more profitable. And it could be operated with fewer headaches."

"You got ideas."

"Well?"

"I'll listen. When? Where?"

"Your place, in an hour."

"You seem to know a lot about me."

"I always check. But I like to talk privately. You understand?"

"There's nobody here but us chickens."

"An hour, then."

Click of the receiver, and silence. Then, through the loud-speaker, Woody's thoughtful, "Well, what do you know? What do you know about that?"

She heard him moving about for a few minutes, and then he went back to the phone and dialed a number. She was waiting with her notebook when the party answered.

"Jimmy?" Woody asked.

"Yeah, me" replied a voice which sounded deliberately disguised.

"Won't see you tonight. Can't make it."

"That leaves me loose, man."

"Can't help it, man. You know how it goes. I'm beat. Gotta stay right here tonight. That's my story. Lay your racket."

"Dug a new disc today. You ever catch Pig-Face on *Any Time, Any Place, Anywhere?*"

"Keep saying."

"Man, when she flats on that line, 'Say the word, you'll be heard, I'll be there ...! You could die, like."

"From Manila, man."

"What?"

"I said, it's a killer. Solid murder. Cool like the chills that kills, see?"

"Oh. I dig."

"Look, you got a chance, pick me up two records, fast."

"Fast, yeah. Don't worry."

"*Ding-Dong Daddy.* I think that's by Pops, but I didn't dig it real good. And *One Hour.* Solid?"

"Crazy. What's that last one?"

"You know—'If I could be with you one hour tonight, If I were free to do the things I might.' "

"Oh, yeah, man. I dig. See you around, man."

"Hope so, man. I sure hope so.

CHAPTER TWENTY-TWO
BIG DEAL

THE HOUSE HAD GROWN strangely quiet. No radios played, no voices were raised in argument. It was almost as though the house itself waited, breathless, the very creaking of its decrepitude hushed. In Peggy's apartment there was only the repressed hum of the loudspeaker, the rustle of her magazine as she unseeingly turned its pages.

Eleven o'clock.

Eleven-five, and eleven-fifteen.

And at eleven-twenty the sound of a buzzer in Woody's kitchen. She heard him go to press the button which would release the latch in the downstairs vestibule. She could even hear the click of the lock two floors below, the light tread on the stairs a moment later.

She was an instant too late in getting to the door and opening it a crack. Whoever it was had already passed along the hall and was on the next staircase. She had a glimpse of black oxfords and gray trouser cuffs.

And she was afraid.

There wasn't any reason to be afraid, she told herself. Someone had come to make a deal with Woody, someone who was himself a criminal and had a proposition to offer. Here was an unexpected opportunity to overhear and record some of the details she needed to know before she could really put her thumb on Woody, squash him like the nasty little insect he was. All she had to do was stay put and quietly listen.

But she was afraid.

She bolted the door and then she went to the recorder and turned down the volume of the speaker. She knew that it could not be heard upstairs at its present level, but she was impelled to quiet it anyway.

"Russell?"

"Yeah."

"I called you."

"Yeah. Come in."

"You're alone?"

"I'm always alone when I talk business."

The sound of footsteps, and then:

"Suppose I look around. Just to be sure. I like to be alone when I talk business, too."

"Go to it, Jack. Knock yourself out. Parlor, bedroom and sink. Make yourself happy."

Peggy crouched over the machine as the footsteps receded and then became louder again.

"No offense. Strictly business. You understand?"

"Strictly business. I like it that way."

"I think we'll get along together."

She knew that voice. She wasn't able to place it yet, because it was distorted by the microphone. But it was familiar. It was …

"Sit down. Unless you want to talk on your feet."

"Thanks. Have one of these?"

"I'll smoke my own."

"Right." A click, a pause, and then, "Can we come directly to the point?"

"You can if you want to. I don't know what your point is."

"Very well. You know me?"

That voice—it was like a name on the tip of one's tongue. She knew it, but … no, it couldn't possibly be …"

"Yes, I know you. At least, I know who you are."

And then Peggy had to admit it to herself. She knew, beyond doubt, who was in the apartment with Woody. She knew, and she could have cried with relief. She wasn't alone, then. She had thought that she was going her own way, working on her own. But all the time, all the time …

"But I haven't been here at all. You understand?"

"So far as I'm concerned, I've just been here by myself in my lonely room."

"Not that it would matter. If I had to, I could prove that I was somewhere else at this moment. *Prove* it. With witnesses, at half a dozen places. But right now I'm at home in my library, reading."

"Okay, okay. What's your pitch?"

"I've been watching your work. Interesting. Very interesting."

"You know what you're talking about? I don't."

"My boy—" And here Peggy could almost see Tom Flanagan settle a bit deeper into the chair, study the cigar he had just lighted. "My boy, I did not come here to play mumblety-peg. I came here to discuss the profitable, but sometimes dangerous business of stealing automobiles for resale."

"Listen, wise guy—"

"No, you listen. I said profitable, and I added dangerous. I know all about the first. As for the second—don't you realize that it is only by an extended run of luck that you have kept out of jail so far? This front of running a car-washing racket that nobody worries about too much—well, I must admit that it shows some forethought for a criminal to disguise himself as a lesser malefactor. Yes, you might be able to cop a plea that way. Once, at least. But the entire idea is fantastic. Only the slightest knowledge of how you run it is enough to make anyone of average intelligence suspicious. That includes police."

"The way I run … Jack, you're tilted on top, ain't you?"

"Turn off that nonsense. Let's get down to cases. You are presently in the business of professional auto theft. Clumsily so. But you're clever. Given direction, you might make a very valuable man."

"Direction? Direction by who?"

"People. People I would designate."

"Look—I'm not admitting anything, see? Not a thing. So far as I'm concerned, you're some flip who stumbled in here. But keep talking."

"I've had my eye on you, Russell. In fact, I might mention in passing that, despite the fact that I am now at home in my library, my present whereabouts are mentioned in an envelope now in the possession of my butler—an envelope which he is instructed to turn over to the police if I do not return at a specified time, and which contains a pretty complete dossier of your activities. That's just in case you might get any ridiculous notion about resorting to violence—"

"Well I'll be damned. I thought it only happened in detective stories. Even a goddamned butler rung in on the act."

"A goddamned good butler," Tom amended. "But what I really have to say is this. Apparently you have a good connection as an outlet. How many cars can they handle a month?"

"I still don't hear you so good. I try, but I just can't make it."

A quick intake of breath as an indication of exasperation, and then Tom said,

"Russell, you're trying my patience. I'm speaking as plainly as possible, and you persist in dodging. Now, to paraphrase a remark made by Joe Louis, maybe you can run, but you can't hide. I have the means of putting you out of business entirely. Of, if you want to be sensible, we can come to an agreement. Which will it be?"

"Let's hear about that last one."

"Very well. Are you authorized to talk about a complete change in the set-up, or is there someone else I have to see?"

"I'm the wheel on this end. How I supply doesn't matter, and you don't have to talk to anybody else because there isn't anybody else to talk to."

"The wheel—but you live in a place like this?"

"You play your way, I'll play mine. I figure this is cool. I know better than to come on like a Midas. I'm stashing now; when my poke is loaded I got plans for things to do and places to do them."

"Thrift and frugality," said Tom, "are qualities much to be admired."

"So admire. Which profile do you want?"

"A bit of spirit, too. I like to see it in a young man."

"Look, I'm not interested in your sex life, or who you like to see it in. Let's get on."

"All right. How many cars can your outlet handle? I asked that before."

"All I can give him. Yells for more."

"Double it?"

"Easy."

"Triple?"

"He'd turn handsprings."

"South American export?"

"Yes, but that's his end. I see that they're cleaned up, he gets first-class merchandise. He pays cash, plus some of the expenses. He kicks, but he comes through."

"Sound operation? No fly-by-night?"

Woody snorted down a laugh.

"If I told you his name … One of the biggest men in New Orleans. It wouldn't surprise me at all you knew each other, going to political conventions and so on."

"Son, I—"

"Don't call me son. Butler or no butler, I get sore easy."

"I've got news for you—son. You've been crowding in a little close. This damned kid gang of yours has got too much attention. It's even been mentioned in the newspapers. People are beginning to talk about car thefts in this town, the insurance rates and so on. Folks never paid attention before. Everything went on quietly. It could go on that way again. You could make twice what you make now. No risks. But you would be working for me."

"Working for you? I don't get it."

"Russell, I always keep several irons in the fire. I have a number of interests we will not discuss tonight, but in which I might find a place for you. The important thing is that you are disturbing one of these interests, at the same time that you have a contact which could actually be valuable in its extension. I know how to use that contact. That's the reason I came to you myself; rather than sending someone else. To be honest, that's the reason I didn't just have you arrested and forget the whole thing. I can use that contact."

To Peggy the conversation had become increasingly more puzzling as it went on. What was Tom's plan, she wondered? What was he doing? It sounded almost as though he meant what he was saying, and was putting through some sort of crooked business deal.

"Only I have to work for you," Woody said.

"Do you have any objection to a police uniform, if the pay is right?"

"Oh. Like that, huh?"

"Yes, probably. Perhaps not. I might use you outside. That depends."

A chill hand reached about Peggy's heart, squeezing out the sense of relief she had felt when she first knew that Tom Flanagan was upstairs.

"I thought you were the Water Commissioner. I didn't know you ran the police too."

"If everybody knew, I wouldn't be," Tom said dryly.

"What's the set-up? How would it work?"

"It's organized and working now. From inside. Suppose you wanted a spotter to line up cars to—ah, merchandise. Who would make a better spotter than a traffic cop? A car is parked overtime; all that may happen is that it's given a green tag. But a city ordinance makes it optional that the car may be towed or driven away. Who would question an officer—except the owner, if he happened to appear suddenly? And he wouldn't have a leg to stand on. The car was illegally parked, and the law is taking its course."

"Well, I'll be damned. I got to hand it to you. Only, one thing—what about the honest johns? Don't they get in the way?"

"Occasionally, but not for long. I know how to handle that. We don't have any trouble."

"Never?"

"We-e-e-ll, hardly ever. But it's always taken care of. You need not worry. I allow nothing—personal friendships, sentimental considerations, or anything else—to interfere with business. You'll be protected."

"That hardly ever stuff—I don't like that. What happens if some rookie gets hot on my tail? What then?"

"Rookie or veteran, it makes no difference. A rookie might be transferred to an outskirt beat. The veteran—well, I recently lost an old and very dear friend on the force. His only vice was an insatiable curiosity concerning matters in which he should have had no interest. Oh, yes—and he was careless with firearms. He had an accident while cleaning a revolver."

"Look, I'm no torpedo. That's strictly for the birds—snowbirds. I've got no gun for hire."

"No one has suggested such a thing. I have often wondered at the stupidity of people who rent such services and thus leave themselves open to all manner of unpleasantness. No, here I believe in the old adage which advises that, wanting a thing done right, one must do it oneself."

Then Peggy knew who had murdered her father.

The details didn't matter. Tom certainly wasn't going to discuss them with Woody anyway. But somehow Mike had got too close to some of Tom's operations.

She could imagine the general pattern. Tom stopping in for a chat about old times and Mike's trouble. And Mike welcoming him. Because, after all, Tom had gone his bail. And then the discussion being led around to Mike's record, his citations, and the engraved citation revolver he had been given a few years ago. Mike bringing out the revolver for Tom to look at. And then, while Tom pretended to examine it …

In the blindness of panicky rage, Peggy lost her head. At the very least, she should have called in for assistance in making the arrest, whatever the charge. And she had no murder charge, of course. She had some shaky recorded evidence of an interstate car racket and a crooked political deal that involved the police force. But, because it was interstate, the Federals would take over. Tom's local influence couldn't help him there. And with Tom unable to get in her way, she might somehow prove that it was he who had killed Big Mike. Yet she did not think of delaying, calling the precinct for aid.

She took her revolver from her purse, checked it, and slipped it into the pocket of the suit she was wearing. With the key to

Woody's apartment in her hand, she opened the door and started up the stairs. She was afraid—as afraid as she had ever been in her life. To strengthen herself, she murmured a phrase over and over:

"For you, Mike. For you."

Irrelevantly, she suddenly realized why Mike had been so secretive about the accident to his finger. Or was it irrelevant? Not as young as he used to be, he knew that someone upstairs—*someone upstairs?*—would use almost any excuse to hasten his retirement, so that he would be out of the way. They were trying to unload him, and he wasn't going to give them the slightest reason to do it!

The key was silent in the lock of Woody's door. She slid her hand into her jacket pocket as she stepped into the tiny foyer. Neither of the two men were aware of her presence until she entered the room in which they were sitting.

"Peggy!" Tom started halfway out of his chair, turned to glance quickly at Woody, and then settled back again. "What the devil are you doing here?"

"Just came to arrest you, Tom. You and Woody."

The door blew closed with a loud snap of the latch. Tom looked at Woody again. Woody shrugged.

"Peggy," Tom said, "I don't know what you're talking about, but whatever it is, this isn't any place for you."

"No, I suppose it isn't, according to your plans. But I'm here. And I know what's going on. I've been listening ever since you arrived."

Tom turned to Woody.

"Is this piece of idiocy your doing?" he asked. "Because—"

"She's Duke Malone's sister," Woody said. "That's all I know."

"Woody isn't involved in my being here," Peggy said. "But he's under arrest along with you, Tom Flanagan."

"Peggy, what do you think you're doing?"

"I'm arresting you. I've been in the apartment downstairs. Since yesterday. There's a microphone in this room, and I've heard everything, so there's no use in trying to talk your way out of this. You! My father's friend. Wanting me to marry you. Talking high principles and lofty sentiments and your sweetness and light all over the place. Well, this is the end of the line. I'm taking you in."

"By God," said Tom, "I really believe you're serious!"

"I never was more so. I told you I've heard everything you two said. And now I understand it all. Not just about the stolen cars and the rest of your rackets. I know that you murdered my father, and I know why. He was catching on to you, and you had to get rid of him to save your skin!"

"Amazing …" Tom said musingly. And then, "Do you think you can prove any of this?"

"I can prove enough to keep you in jail long enough for me to get the whole story. Every word that's been said here tonight, and that's being said now, is on a tape recorder downstairs."

"I see. Then I'll have to do something about that, won't I?"

He started to rise, and then Peggy's revolver was in her hand.

"Just stay where you are, Mr. Flanagan. I have a call to Headquarters to make."

She sidled toward the phone, keeping both of the men in view and firing range.

And Tom laughed.

"Don't carry it any farther, Peg. Put that toy down. And don't go any nearer the phone."

"This toy is real, mister. It shoots and it can kill, and I know how to use it."

"Yes?" Now Tom stood up. He carefully laid his cigar in a tray, and then took a step toward her.

"I'm warning you, Tom. I'll fire if I have to. Sit down. And don't *you* get any funny ideas about a fast move, either, Woody."

Tom chuckled. Took another step.

"Pull the trigger," he suggested. "Just to see what happens."

"No closer, Tom. I've told you twice."

"Yes, you've told me. And now I'm going to tell you something. That thing you're holding in your hand is somewhat less effective than a child's water-gun. Why? Because the cartridges in it hold no powder. It occurred to me some time ago that there was more motivation behind your desire to get on the police force than you were admitting. The possibility that you might stumble upon something—as you have—was something I considered. It seemed wiser, in view of this, to clip your claws beforehand, just in case you might come to my house some night to shoot me, rather than sleep with me."

He smiled and went on,

"Last time you were on the firing range, you were given a new issue of ammunition when you finished up, weren't you? Well, that was by my order. That revolver won't fire, Peggy. Try it. If you're afraid to aim it at me, point it out the window, at the wall. It doesn't matter. I'm taking it away from you in either case."

He moved toward her. She backed off a step. Was he bluffing? She didn't want to shoot him. She didn't want to shoot anybody. There was time for a quick snap shot toward the window—

And the hammer fell with a sharp, empty click.

"Too bad," Tom said. "Too bad you weren't either a little bit smarter or a little bit more stupid."

He wrested the revolver from her hand as she stared at it, dropped it into his pocket, and glanced quickly at Woody, who had been sitting frozenly under its threat. At no time had Tom had his back to the other man, and he was careful to keep him under observation even as he took Peggy's wrist and gently led her away from the phone.

He led her gently by the wrist, and turned her to face him again in the middle of the room.

And then he slapped her across the mouth with all his strength.

The blow knocked her to her knees, and he struck her again, his open hand fanning backward and forward across her cheeks half a dozen times before she could bury her face in her hands. Trembling with shock, she remained there on the floor as he stepped back. A soft sob escaped her, and then tears began to fall through her spread fingers.

"Hey—" Woody began.

"Stay where you are, Russell." Tom's hand slipped into his jacket, beneath the armpit, and reappeared holding his own revolver. "I don't want things to get any more messy than they are already."

Woody settled back in the chair, his eyes on the blue-steel gun barrel which had swung his way. Tom picked up his cigar and sat down on the arm of the sofa, where he studied the glowing ash.

"We appear to be," he finally said, "in some difficulty. A grave difficulty. I see no solution which does not involve a large measure of unpleasantness for all of us."

Peggy looked up at him through her tears. "You murderer! And my father was supposed to be your oldest friend!"

"I was sorry about that, Peggy. Sorry long before it happened. There just wasn't any other way. I've wanted to make it up to you and the boy."

"You admit it then! You admit that you shot him!"

"It had to be that way, finally, Peg. I didn't want it like that, and I did my best to avoid it."

"Did your best—like arranging a frame-up, to try to get him thrown off the force! Do you admit that, too?"

"That's not quite how it worked. I—Russell, I've warned you to stay put!"

"I don't like this. I don't want to have anything to do with this," Woody said.

"Can't say that I blame you. Damned unfortunate situation for you. Obviously, you have heard too much. Learned far more than I can afford to have any man know about me. No fault of yours, either. Sorry, I'd hoped that we could do business."

"Man, I don't know what you're talking about. But I just wish you would both go some place else. I don't like guns. If you two have a hassle, take it out of here. I don't need it. To hell with business. I'm leaving town anyway."

"I'm afraid not, Russell. You're not stupid. Not at all as stupid as you would like to have people believe. You know that I wouldn't dare now to allow you to leave town—or this room. Either of you."

"What—what is he saying?" Peggy turned from Tom to Woody, and then looked back at Tom's revolver.

"What he's saying," Woody told her, "isn't the best. He's talking about a rub, chicken, and I don't see where I fit in. I don't know anything, I haven't heard anything, I don't want to hear anything. All I want it to grab my bag and blow town. I know when to keep my mouth shut if I hear anything, which I haven't."

Tom smiled, but shook his head.

"I'm sorry, Russell. I can't take that chance. It's not that I bear you any ill will. At most, you've only been a nuisance. But I think it will be better this way anyhow. Things will get back to normal, go on as they always have. I like to live a quiet, conservative life."

"You think I'm just going to sit here and take it?"

"Have you any choice? One move in the wrong direction, and you get a bullet in the face immediately. My way—well, there is always the possibility that I might change my mind at the last minute … isn't there?"

"By God, I think you're crazy!"

"My boy, I wouldn't deny it."

"You'll never get away with it. Start shooting in here and you'll have the whole house yelling for cops before you make it to the door."

"Wrong, son. Possibly you have never seen one of these." From his pocket he took a length of perforated tubing which, without taking his eyes from Woody, he quickly fitted over the muzzle of the revolver. "A silencer. Of course, all it can possibly do is cut down the report, not really silence it. But it's quite efficient. The neighbors will not be disturbed."

"And that, I suppose," Peggy hissed at him like a defiant cat, "is what you used to kill my father!"

"As a matter of fact, no. I've never used it, except in practice. I really don't understand, Peggy, where you ever got the notion that I'm a cold-blooded, professional killer. Other than Mike, I've killed only one man in my life, and that was in the old days—and besides, it was an accident."

"You really did use his own gun, then. That wasn't just another piece of hocus-pocus you fixed up?"

She was trying to get his attention more fully upon herself. Woody was no friend, but they were in this together, now. Given a chance, Woody might, under the impetus of desperation, take a chance on attacking Tom. After that …

"I suppose it doesn't matter if you know now. And I'd like you to know, at least, that it wasn't something I'd planned. As you've guessed, Mike was getting in my way. He'd been on the force a long time and knew his way around; he wasn't blind. First

I tried kicking him upstairs—arranged to have him promoted to a job behind a desk, where he could take things easy and not be underfoot. He refused the promotion. I tried to have him retired on ill health or disability. That didn't work. I had people offer him good jobs outside, and he turned them down. At last there was nothing to do but get him dropped. *Put your hand back on the chair arm, Russell!"*

"'Yeah. Yeah, sure," Woody said, as the revolver swung his way again. "Just got a cramp in my shoulder."

"A horse room was opened behind a cigar store on his beat," Tom went on, "by arrangement with a nasty little person who had been willing to do a small stretch for a price and some promises. Mike reported it at once, and was told merely to keep an eye on it while detectives tried to get full evidence on the syndicate behind it. After that he was given to understand that the force had managed to plant a man on the inside. So he wasn't very much surprised, I suppose, when a fellow looking more like a plainclothesman than a plainclothesman does, stopped him on the street to ask directions and then muttered that Mike was to stop in the tobacco store and buy a cigar, at which time the clerk would give him an envelope to take back to the station house. And that's when they cracked down."

"Then why did you kill him?" Peggy asked. "You had him where you wanted him!"

"Because things had gone too far, damn it! I'd given him too much time while I was trying to ease him out. From a couple of things he said that night when I went to visit him, I realized that he knew more about the set-up than I'd thought. He hadn't actually figured me in yet, but in the direction he was working it was only a matter of time. And it seemed that he might even then be beginning to be suspicious of me; he was reluctant about answering some questions I asked.

"I was carrying my own revolver, but I thought I saw a way of making it look like suicide, and I managed to persuade him to bring out his own. He is—was—very proud of that gun, you know. But it was empty when he handed it to me. I hinted something about a drink, and he went to the kitchen. While he was gone I unloaded mine and used its cartridges to load his. He came back, and then …

"Well, that shot was loud as hell, but no one investigated. If they had, I planned to say I'd been in the bathroom and had just found him. Then I threw out the drinks, put the glasses away, and arranged things as they were found later. I left thinking I'd done a fairly thorough job. Apparently I had not. As a matter of curiosity, Peg, what set you off on this insane detection spree?"

"The gun. It hung from his finger. A broken finger that could never have pulled a trigger."

"Ah! I thought it was a bit odd when I saw the pictures. When I left him, I had clasped his hand about the gun and then allowed his hand to fall over the side of the chair as naturally as possible. I noticed, of course, that the gun did not drop, and I assumed that his finger remained in that position because of some temporary nervous spasm which would soon relax. Since naturalism was my entire objective, I did not disturb it. But I am afraid we waste time. We have other matters at hand, haven't we?"

"Now look," Woody said. He was sweating now, and had begun to chew at his lip. "Now, look, there doesn't have to be any rough stuff. All I want is a chance to blow town. So far as I'm concerned, I never met you, I never saw you. Just a bus ticket, that's all I need. To hell with the bus ticket. I'll walk. I'll walk out of here right now, and you'll never see or hear from me again. All I was doing was sitting here minding my own business when you called me up and all this started. But that's all right. I don't mind. Just let me walk to that door. All I want is out."

"Stand up, Peggy," Tom said, ignoring him.

"Tom ... You can't. You just can't mean it."

"Damn it, get on your feet when I tell you to! Do you think I'm happy about the way things have turned out? Why couldn't you have married me when I asked you to? At least a wife can't testify against her husband, and maybe I could have gotten you interested in something more womanly than running around playing cops-and-robbers."

Fresh tears started down Peggy's cheeks as she slowly crept to her feet.

She looked despairingly at Woody, who sat tensely hunched in his chair. There was no help in that direction. He would not even try to save himself. She was alone, as all must be alone, finally, in the face of death. And she could not even be brave.

"You don't have to kill him, Tom. Woody won't talk. He just wants to get as far away from this as possible." She had clasped her hands before her like a little girl at prayer. "As for me," she stalled desperately, "you don't have to kill me either. I could go back to Paris and stay there and never bother you." She didn't really mean it, any more than she meant her next words. "Why— I'll do anything ... I'm afraid, Tom. I'm afraid!"

He looked at her with a strange expression, seeming to be weighing something in his mind.

"Anything ..." he said beneath his breath.

She grasped at the straw desperately.

"Whatever you say, Tom. It will all be just as you say."

"Beginning now? As of this minute?" he asked in a curious tone.

"Beginning now. I swear!"

"And you'll do exactly as I say, without question?"

"No questions, Tom."

"I don't believe you. But very well—we shall see. First of all, take off your clothes."

She looked from him to Woody, down whose face perspiration was now pouring in rivulets.

"You want me to—in front of …?"

"I thought you said no questions! Yes. All of them. You can just drop them where you stand, for now."

She did not question, but she stared at him. Could he have gone mad, suddenly? Or had he been cunningly insane, all the time she had known him? And what did that insanity hold in store for her?

"Well?"

"Yes, Tom. Of course."

The other way death waited.

She could feel Woody's eyes upon her, although she did not even glance at him as, garment by garment, she stripped to nakedness before the two men. Tom's vigilance did not waver, even though he watched Peggy, no slightest move of Woody's escaped him. When the final silken bit of underclothing had fallen with the rest, he studied her for a moment with an expression that was almost sad, almost tender. Then he said,

"Go over to Russell and sit on his lap."

"I—yes, Tom."

She crossed the room and did as he had ordered.

"Not that way. Put your arms around him and curl up against him. What's the matter, Russell? Don't you know what to do with a naked woman?"

"He's insane," Peggy whispered against Woody's ear as he drew her closer.

"I heard that," Tom said. "But what I'm doing is really very sensible." He stepped toward the open window which fronted on the fire escape. "You see, now, we have a charming little love scene set up—one which is being reenacted in many a living room at this moment, I am sure. It is exactly the sort of situation which a certain type of voyeuristic maniac looks for—to destroy. Every week or so you come across some mention of this in the papers. The parked car in Lovers' Lane, the two embracing lovers shot or bludgeoned to death. Why? I don't know. But I know that those killers prowl the city, peering into windows, climbing fire-escapes …

"And so it will appear that this is what has happened tonight. The act of a nameless madman. I am sorry that I had to trick you, Peggy. I have really enjoyed you very much, and I do not want to hurt you. And don't worry about Duke. I'll see to it that he gets straightened out. If you just sit very quietly, as you are, you will feel nothing."

Standing at the window, he raised the revolver.

There were two shots.

Almost the last thing Peggy knew, as she whirled into blackness, was the sound of Woody's voice.

"You sure took your goddamned time about it," he said.

And then,

"Play it cool, man," came the answer.

That was John Fanson.

CHAPTER TWENTY-THREE
WITH PASSION

THEY SAT AROUND the table in the modest dining room of the flat three nights later—Peggy, John Fanson, Duke, Woody, and Officer Ada Granados.

"More spaghetti, somebody?" Peggy urged. "Woody, you look as though you could make it. You scoffin' light to be polite, man?"

Ada laughed as Woody declined.

"It sounds so funny, coming from you, Peggy," she said, holding her glass out toward the Chianti bottle which Duke was offering. "All out of character. Like Woody being an F.B.I. man. I'd never spot him for that. But see here—I was promised the whole story after dinner, and as far as I'm concerned, dinner is over."

"I'll get coffee up," Peggy said. "No, sit still, all of you. I like to work my own way. I'll take care of these things. In the meantime, you men can brief this curious colleague of mine."

She began gathering the dishes, and Ada looked at Woody, who looked at John Fanson, who looked at Duke, who looked back at Woody.

"Well," Woody said, "it all began—my end of it, that is—with the insurance companies. They'd been worrying for some time about the high car-theft rate in this town, and their investigators weren't getting far. They had enough to suspect a ring that was working interstate, if not internationally. And they were getting damned little cooperation from the local police, in a polite sort of way. And there were hints of other complications—gambling, some unstamped liquor moving around, things like that. Enough to make it seem worth a Federal job."

He snatched a piece of hard bread from the plate for which Peggy was reaching, dipped it quickly through the sauce remaining at the bottom of the bowl, and popped it into his mouth. He chewed thoughtfully at it until Peggy had left for the kitchen.

"Just about the same time," he then went on, "Mike Malone came to the offices of the F.B.I. and told a story which tied in. He was certain that the police force was corrupt, and that crime was being tolerated, and probably also participated in, by those higher up. He couldn't make a complaint within the department, obviously, so he was bringing us the information he had. That information dovetailed with what we already knew, and he was told to go on as he had been doing, to make a report to the F.B.I. whenever he ran into anything new, and that an investigation would be started from our end. Then—he was killed. That wasn't anybody's fault. Until then no one had realized just how serious things were."

"I've seen some damned strange stuff myself," Ada said. "But every time you try to get your hands on it, there isn't anything there."

"You won't see that any longer," John Fanson put in. "This shake-up in the department goes all the way to the top. When Tom Flanagan thought he was dying, he began to sing loud and strong."

"That isn't going to help him, is it?" Duke asked. "I mean, he won't be able to cop a plea on the murder charge just for turning State's evidence on that other stuff?"

"Pretty bitter, aren't you, fellow?" John said.

"You're damned right I'm bitter. Wouldn't you be?"

"I guess I would. Well, the best he can do is beat the chair. With what they have on him now, plus what they collect every day when one or another of his stooges blabs to save his own skin, I don't think we'll be seeing Mr. Flanagan again."

"Yeah? What about influence? You know how much weight he pushes. It isn't just in the city. It goes straight to the state capitol. You've seen pictures of him and the Governor with their arms over each other's shoulders, all buddy-buddy."

"I could give you an argument right there," John replied. "But I'll concede the point. So he's got the governor. How much higher do you suppose his influence extends?"

"I don't see that it has to go much higher."

"All right. Now I'll tell you something the doctors found out while they were patching him up. Tom Flanagan has a brain tumor. Inoperable. They give him four months to live. Whom is he going to see, and make a deal with, about that?"

"You mean there isn't anything they can do?"

"Not a thing, in his case. It's gone too far. That explains a lot of things, doesn't it? He just hasn't been sane a large part of the time."

"Like when he killed Mike."

"Yes. Like when he killed Mike. He's been sick, Duke."

"Sick like a mad dog. What do you do with a mad dog? You destroy it, get rid of it."

"I guess," John Fanson said, "that it's out of our hands now, isn't it?"

Woody broke in on the silence that followed. "Anyway, I was sent in to look things over. Peg had just joined the force, for reasons that were pretty obvious. Since we were sure that whoever was responsible for Mike's death would be keeping an eye on Peggy, we felt that we could get at him through her. A bit of competition in the car racket looked like the easiest way. The way it was finally arranged, it took Peggy's attention away from a direct attempt to investigate her father's death on her own, and it thereby lulled the wariness of the murderer—at the same time that it laid out the bait for him to show himself. I got next to Duke, here—no easy job, because he thought I was the original zoot-suit kid and wouldn't have anything to do with me until I took him down to the Bureau and let him read some testimony his father had given us—and we went to work."

Duke looked embarrassed. "All right. You don't have to rub it in."

"I wasn't putting you down, Jackson. You came on straight. You want a job when you finish school, you know it's lying there."

"What language," Ada asked John, "is this man's native tongue?"

"Harvardese, as spoken in the early forties, I should say."

"Two kinds coffee!" Peggy called from the kitchen. "Watered-down American, or the real stuff?"

The vote was unanimous for the real stuff.

"What was this gaff you had with the kids?" Ada wanted to know. "Peggy started to tell me when we were making the salad, but the pasta boiled over and I didn't get it right."

"Those kids, along with their parents," Woody said, "are going to have a little talking-to. Because of the way this town was drifting, there were dozens of kid gangs, so we used one of them to fight the very situation that created them. The cars they picked up and moved around were all either official cars, rented jobs, or cars belonging to people on the Bureau. Take one car, let six different kids shuffle it from one spot to another during the day, and so far as they are concerned they have handled six cars. We depended on that last idea getting to Peggy through some of the leaks we deliberately opened, and from Peggy to the parties we thought would be interested. There were faked items in gossip columns, a general whispering campaign was set up to make the whole thing seem bigger than it was, and Duke went into a big act around the house."

"Yeah, but was it hard to get her to move the way we wanted her to!" Duke said. "Three times I drove a car right out in front of her nose before she arrested me. Never even saw me. And when I planted that letter in the kitchen that made it seem that Woody was heading a big deal, with a plant in New Jersey and all—I wasn't even sure that she had read it next morning when I picked it up again, even though I had it lying there in a certain way. And then she balled that up. What cooperation!"

"What Duke means," Woody explained, "is that we had hoped the mention of the empty apartment below mine would smoke out the fox we were after. He was being slow in showing himself, and we thought that he might come around to rent the place, just to try to get a line on me. Of course it never was advertised. The superintendent had his orders, and we were all set to put in mikes and a phone tap if we got any action. If no one was interested, that would indicate either that Peggy wasn't passing on the information we were planting for her, or that the whole idea was flopping. Then *she* walked in, put a tap on my phone, and a bug—a mike—in my living room. It *was* a ball-up, from there on."

"You suspected Flanagan, then?"

"Yes, among others. From what Mike had given us, and with what we'd learned since, he was top man on our list. By the time he called me to make the appointment, I knew that the phone was cut into Peg's, and I'd found the bug she'd wired. That was why I had to talk with Fanson in a kind of double-talk when I called him."

"I should have thought," Ada said, "that you'd have had a stake-out with at least half a dozen men, instead of just one."

"If I had to go through that again, I'd have two dozen. But it seemed that it was just a feeler on Flanagan's part, that it really wasn't time to make the pinch. I just wanted somebody around for company, in case something went wrong—as it did. I was pretty sure that it was Flanagan who'd phoned, and I was also pretty sure he was a killer. I get lonesome on a job like that."

"You been with the F.B.I. long, John?" Duke asked.

John grinned at him.

"He's done a couple of jobs for us," Woody said. "He's getting material for a book called, 'I Was a Cop for the F.B.I.'"

Peggy reappeared with a tray bearing the coffee service.

"And then," she said, having heard the last few words, "I went upstairs to be a heroine."

"Shortly after which," John added, taking a cup from the tray and managing to spill some of it, "I came around to case things, found her door ajar, and went in, where I listened for a while to some very interesting things on that sound-system she had rigged up. I'd learned that morning that she had the apartment, and the way Woody talked on the phone tipped me off that his line was tapped, so I wasn't too surprised to find that. Then things started to get rough."

"You took your time," Woody said. "You sure took your time."

"I couldn't help it, man," John protested. "You get out on that fire-escape sometime and see how things lay out from there. I was there for fifteen minutes, at least, and I couldn't angle in. First of all, I couldn't just start climbing in the window while he held that roscoe. I couldn't get a clean shot at him, either. And he was holding that thing on both of you.

I knew you were sweating, but I couldn't do a damned thing about it. You hadn't even unlocked the bedroom window."

"Well, you could have whistled like a hoot owl or something, just to let me know you were there. That would have been something. The way things were, I didn't have a chance to go for any iron."

"What do you mean," Duke asked, " 'The way things were?' "

Woody and John looked at each other, but not at Peggy. She looked at both of them and then bent over her coffee.

"Nothing," Woody said. "I mean, I didn't have a chance to make a move. He had the—the drop on me."

"Twice," John said hurriedly, "I was ready to take a chance on his wrist. But it was too big a chance, when I had the gun up. I had to wait."

"Not the third time, though," Duke told Ada. "The wrist first and then the shoulder. Pretty good. And when he saw himself bleeding, he though he was going to die. He was sure he'd been lunged, and when they got him to the hospital—"

"Could we, perhaps, talk about something else for a while?" Peggy suggested.

And, for the remainder of the time that they were at the table, they found other subjects of discussion. Afterward, Ada insisted upon doing the dishes, and recruited Woody as assistant, while John and Peggy and Duke played a fast game of Scrabble. Ada and Woody came into the living room just as the game was finishing. Ada looked rather flushed.

"If no one minds," she said, "Woody and I thought we might take in a movie. There's just about time to make the late show."

"Mind?" Duke said. "Why should we? What show is it? Maybe I—"

Peggy dug him hard in the ribs, and he subsided.

"Crazy," he finished.

As Ada and Woody were preparing to leave, he looked at his watch.

"Just remembered something. I've got to cut, too."

And so John and Peggy were finally alone. The flat was very quiet for a while, and then John asked,

"When?"

"Any time, John. If you still want me now. I've told you all about Tom and me. I can't apologize for that. I don't even try to excuse myself. That was it, and it happened."

"Do you think I've been a saint all my life? Do you think that most people, in learning, don't make mistakes? That won't be our problem—if we must have a problem."

"Another problem we won't have is me trying to be a cop. I can't do it, John. I don't want it."

"I guess one cop in the family is enough. Shall we go to the License Bureau tomorrow?"

"Yes."

"And then what?"

"Whatever—no. Let's go to France. Can we afford France?"

"If we squeeze. So we'll go to France. I've always wanted to."

She drew away from him, shaking out her hair, which was now somewhat disarranged.

"I just thought of something. Loose ends lying around. I've mentioned Jacques …"

He nodded.

"I did a lousy thing to him. He loved me, John. All right? Understand?"

"Yes."

"And when I came back here, he wrote to me. There's a letter somewhere that I haven't even opened, much less answered. I think I'd better do something about that. It just isn't … it …"

"I understand."

It took her several minutes to find the letter. She tore it open, quickly read it short message. John interested himself in his fingernails. When she had finished, she handed it to him.

"Dear Peggy," he read. *"I hope you are happy. When you read this, I am afraid I'll be an old married man. This is a sudden thing to you, I am fearful, but it is, as they say in the American fashion, just one of those things. Life must go on, is it not the way? Matters come to their conclusion, and there is a sadness always, but a new beginning and a rebirth.*

You would care about Marie. She is interested in things and laughs often. Her family is in silks. It was something arranged between her folks and mine, to be truthful.

I hope that you will come to visit us when you have a chance.

And I hope that you are very happy and will not forget old times.

With passion,
Jacques."

Peggy laughed as John handed back the letter.

"Shall we go to your place?" she asked.

END